HAUNTED BACKROADS:

GHOSTS OF WESTFIELD

BY
NICOLE R. KOBROWSKI

UNSEENPRESS.COM, INC.
WESTFIELD, INDIANA

Library of Congress Cataloging-in-Publication Data

Kobrowski, Nicole
   Haunted Backroads: Ghosts of Westfield
         Includes index
   1. Ghosts Indiana; 2. Paranormal Indiana ; 3. Indiana History; 4. Indiana Travel

Library of Congress Control Number: 2008930458
ISBN-978-0-9774130-3-4
ISBN-0-9774130-3-9

Printed in the United States of America

Published by
Haunted Backroads Books
an imprint of Unseenpress.com, Inc.
PO Box 687
Westfield, IN 46074

Although the authors and publisher have made every effort to ensure the accuracy and completeness of information contained in this book, we assume no responsibility for errors, inaccuracies, omissions or any inconsistency herein. Any slights of people, places or organizations are unintentional.

Cover design by Brittany A. Norris and Nicole R. Kobrowski
Logo by Lorri A. Kennedy
Text layout and design by Unseenpress.com, Inc.
Additional font work by Chad Savage
Edited by Paula Dunn and Michael Kobrowski
Cover photograph by Nicole R. Kobrowski

All photos unless otherwise indicated are property of Unseenpress.com, Inc.

NOTES

The persons, events, places and incidents depicted in this book are based on oral history, memoirs, interviews and accounts that were used as research for this book. The author makes no claim as to the veracity of the information. The author makes no claim as to the exact historical authenticity of the legends presented in this book. The author does not guarantee any location directions contained in this book and you visit these sites at your own risk. Although many sites are open to visitors during the day (and some in the evening), they all have owners.

Additionally, this book is comprised of material that is intended for the entertainment of its readers. The author has paid particular attention to collecting legends that have been told, in many cases, for generations. The information concerning these legends may not reflect historical events. The author takes no responsibility for the veracity of each story except that she believes the storytellers. The author has attempted to research each area as accurately as possible.

Although we made every effort to ensure that the information was correct at the time the book went to press, we do not assume and hereby disclaim any liability to any party for loss, damage, or injury caused by information contained in this book. Furthermore the publishers disclaim any liability resulting from the use of this book. The publishers and author do not condone, advise, or recommend visiting these sites without obtaining permission first and taking safety precautions.

We apologize if there is inaccurate information presented in the book and will rectify future additions and editions if we are contacted by mail or e-mail and provided the correct information.

Other Titles by Nicole Kobrowski

Distance Learning: A Guide to System Planning and Implementation
(by Merrill, Young, and Kobrowski)

Haunted Backroads: Central Indiana (and other stories)

The Encyclopedia of Haunted Indiana

The following titles are published by Kieser Verlag (Bildungsverlag EINS):

Metal Line
Hotel Line (Instructor's Guide)
Englisch für Elektroberufe
Supply Line
Construction Line

Future Titles:
The Shadows of Central State Hospital: A Mental Health Legacy
The Encyclopedia of Haunted Indiana (2nd Ed.)

DEDICATION

As always, this book is dedicated to my family, who is my heart and soul.

Additionally, this book is dedicated to Kelly Ann Fleming, a young writer whose brilliant voice was abruptly silenced one unspeakable spring day.

ABOUT THE AUTHOR

Nicole Kobrowski is the co-owner of Unseenpress.com, Inc., which was founded in 2001. She and her husband Michael started the business because of their interest in the paranormal and their love of history. She has written professionally under a variety of pen names for over 20 years, including books for ESL and dozens of articles on a myriad of topics. Being a paranormal enthusiast for over 25 years, she has done investigation work in many areas including spirit photography, electronic voice phenomenon, and automatic writing. In addition to her work in the paranormal field, Nicole is an Educational Consultant and teaches at IUPUI. Currently, she lives in her "über" haunted home with her husband and two children.

PRIVACY AND POLICIES

We do not condone or encourage any type of harassment, vandalism, unauthorized cemetery preservation, or unauthorized trespassing. This type of thrill seeking only garners an unsavory pall over the paranormal community.

We are responsible in our investigations and research with integrity and according to scientific principles and standards.

We follow strict research and privacy guidelines. We reserve the right not to publish names and places contained within our books. Names denoted with an asterisk (*) in this book have been changed to honor the privacy of the participants.

We endeavor to create a true learning community for paranormal investigations with a collaborative spirit by partnering with responsible organizations that promote similar goals.

TABLE OF CONTENTS

INTRODUCTION

This book represents part of my home for the last 11 years. When Michael and I moved back from Germany in 2000, we were both a bit adrift. Finding where we fit into Indiana's landscape was important to us. I had lived in Indiana my whole life, previous to my departure from Germany.

When we had the opportunity to move to Westfield, we never dreamed it would feel so much like home. Michael had been born and raised in Germany, and admittedly sat the Jewish-German fence for the majority of his life. When he visited Indiana, he fell in love with the cornfields, barns and the pace. Even though he was raised in Nuremberg, a city of 500,000 people, the mentality of the Germans and the pace of life for the most part is very similar to Indiana. I guess I was lucky his visits were before the snow fell, the tornados blew through, and the scorching heat baked us!

Westfield is a wonderful mix of tradition and treasure. Our claim to fame is the Underground Railroad. Yet, the every-day lives of the people who live(d) here are fascinating stories in themselves- with or without the ghosts. The stories contained in this volume come from our investigations, our research and our tours. These stories are some of our favorite ghosts and represent the rich history behind Westfield, the different groups of people who live(d) here, and Hamilton County. Although Camilla Axelrod might consider me "transient" still, I feel like Westfield is home.

I am pleased to be the first author to write a book about the paranormal in Hamilton County. It is meant to encompass as much as I was able to put in this version. I had to cut the cord somewhere!

Use this book for fun. Use it to explore beautiful Hamilton County. Decide for yourself if you believe. But most of all, I hope you enjoy it.

As always, I thank the many researchers, friends, ghost hunters and people who have entrusted their stories to me. I especially thank Michael, my friend and partner, and Paula Dunn, who is an unbelievably kind, smart, and funny person. I also want to thank the generous support of the Westfield Washington Historical Society.

In this particular book, because of the sensitive nature of some stories, we've changed names to protect privacy. While it seems people are now ok to go on a ghost tour or paranormal investigation, they are still somewhat worried about appearing "nuts".

It's been a long time in finishing this book and every moment has been a labor of love- or something like that (at times). As I write this, I am enjoying a gorgeous Spring day in my writing nook, looking at a weeping willow next to a pond and listening to the melodic rock of Night Ranger's newest CD. Life couldn't be better.

Happy Nightscares!

Nicole Kobrowski
June 2011

MARLOW'S CAFE

112 East Main Street

When the plain, frame building on Main Street was built, the town probably had more on their minds than just ghosts. The Knights of Pythias meeting house was upstairs. The Knight of Pythias boast of members who are upstanding citizens and who try to impart good will and help to all they meet in life. H.L. Boyd's Grocery was downstairs, rumored to be somewhat unkempt and a place to loaf more than conduct business. It was a time when people cared about their community and neighbors, and they took time to better the lives of the people around them. Later, Horton's Meat Market and Daugherty's Coffee Shop moved in downstairs. This building was a place of business and of charity, much as it is today.

Today, the building is home to Marlow's Café. A cozy place to be sure, the Marlow family has a history of its own. In 1939, the original Marlow's Café sat at the corner of West 38th Street and Illinois in Indianapolis. Frank and Mary Marlow, the original owners, served up homemade breakfast, lunch, and dinner. They were famous all over the city for their family recipe sausage gravy (which is still used today). The couple worked hard, as anyone in the restaurant industry knows, often coming in well before 5:30 am prepping food for the day- cutting vegetables, making soups, and baking pies and cakes. Sometimes the couple left the business late in the evening. Still, the restaurant provided a comfortable living for Mary and Frank, and they raised three girls and one boy while in Indianapolis.

Later in life, they moved the café to Westfield, and in 1975 Marlow's was opened at its current location. Frank and Mary Marlow wanted a smaller, country feel for their business and they weren't disappointed. The café sported a 20 person counter and the Marlows kept an immaculate kitchen. After 38 years in the business, Frank and Mary retired. Ever the businessman, Frank sold the café to his only son Bob, who has run it ever since. In 1980 Bob married Annette, who became his partner in the family legacy.

Annette has had her own set of paranormal experiences in her life. As a teenager of 14 living in Indianapolis, she seriously considered sleeping in the same bed as her parents after she had her first experi-

Marlow's Cafe on Main Street. The best iced tea in Hamilton County is always plentiful and chat with the Marlow's and regulars is always friendly.

ence walking down the stairs. Late one night, she walked downstairs to visit the rest room. She saw a figure at the edge of the staircase. She also heard strange noises in the attic that moved her downstairs so quickly even her grandmother took notice.

As an adult, Annette continued to experience paranormal events. Once while living in Indianapolis, she had a dream that her son hurt himself giving him a head injury. She woke up crying. As she related the story to Bob, she heard her son crying. Apparently he had jumped off the couch, hitting his head and giving him an injury that required stitches.

When the Marlow's lived in the South Harbor subdivision in Noblesville, Annette experienced unexplained events. When the family moved in, they installed a shelf in the kitchen, secured by toggle bolts. One night about a week later, they woke up to a loud crash- almost the sound of someone breaking in. Rushing to the scene, they found the shelf sitting on the floor, its contents lying broken around it. Both Bob and Annette felt as if something didn't want them there- or was at least unhappy with the remodeling they were doing. To Annette the event became clear when a little neighbor girl asked them why they were cutting down a tree. The girl told Annette it had been planted in memory of a former owner's dead relative. However, Bob and Annette remained in the home- only to experience more activity.

Another time, Bob was out of town golfing. Annette was with her daughter eating dinner in the kitchen. From the next room, they heard the sound of someone using Bob's putter. Both women looked at each other and said, "Did you hear that?" They clung to each other for a short time and finally went into the room. The putter was where it should have been, leaning against the fireplace with golf balls next to it. The women remained on edge the entire weekend. When Bob heard about it, he joked, "It must be Frank."

Throughout their time in the home, they experienced more events, such as feeling someone was standing next to the bed or hearing footsteps throughout the house when no one was at home.

But for Annette life was not just the paranormal. She raised two boys and two girls and enjoyed the work at the cafe. Even the children would occasionally wash dishes and her oldest daughter, Holly, started waiting tables at 13. Although she admits, "Working with my husband behind the grill is sometimes challenging", she also states with a smile that she finds working at Marlow's a "good experience most of the time".

Annette says she enjoys her work because she likes getting to know people. The majority of her customers are friendly and she says "It's fun serving and seeing people happy."

Apparently some people are still very happy to be at Marlow's.

In 1977, Bob bought the building from the Knights of Pythias and turned the upper floor into offices. A tenant moved in and turned the area into cubicles, installing high walls to section off the space. Annette tells the story:

> *"One late evening my renter was working alone. However, something was in the next cubical rolling around in the office chair. She hesitated to check it out, but wanted to be sure her employees had gone home for the day.*
>
> *Finding no one, she was certain it was a ghost. She came to see us the very next day to inform us of her evening. Our renter said, "Do you know you have a ghost?"*
>
> *I'm still not comfortable going upstairs sometimes by myself."*

And with good reason. Annette has had her own experiences in the building- strange happenings which are very much unexplained. One day, as she was standing at a sink in the back corner of the kitchen washing pots and pans, Annette felt someone standing directly behind her in the small space- pulling her apron strings!

Annette turned to face the prankster, expecting it to be her daughter but no one was there. When she told her family of the experience both of her daughters said they had the same feeling and experiences on more than one occasion. Later that same day, Lindsay, one of Annette's daughters, experienced the same event and same results. Holly always wondered if it was her grandfather Frank (who had passed on by this time) continuing to pay visits to the café.

Bob Marlow, however, isn't as accepting of the events as his wife and daughters. He was a skeptic for a long time, until one night he had a shared experience with his wife. Bob's parents, Frank and Mary passed on within three months of each other. Dealing with a parent's death is not easy for most people, and Bob was no exception. The months following his parents' deaths were emotional. One night soon after his mother died, Bob and Annette fell into bed exhausted. Later that night both sat straight up and looked at each other with wide eyes and said, "Do you hear that?"

Bob asked, "What do you hear?"

"Coins dropping on the dresser." Annette replied.

The chilling part of this story is that the couple did have a bowl with change in it on the dresser. They described the sound as someone "scooping up" the coins, tossing them and pinging them into the bowl. The couple had always heard of coin movement being an old wives' tale indicating the presence of a recently deceased family member. That night they stayed awake talking, although Annette admits she stayed awake much longer then Bob did!

From that point, Bob said he was still a skeptic, but with rules. He believes in the paranormal, but only when certain rules apply to ghosts. He believes spirits can indicate their presence, such as family watching over loved ones, but that they cannot physically show their presence.

People who remember Frank Marlow, remember he was very focused on what he did well- running a business and serving his customers. He was said to have had a "way" of ringing the bell in his café that signaled food was up and ready to be served. People remember his ringing to be somewhat sharp and loud, because he believed customers needed to be served food the way it was meant- hot and filling.

Maybe he's still on the job. In addition to presences, pulled apron strings, and rolling chairs, the folks at Marlow's Café experience other disturbing occurrences- all blamed on Frank, or at least a ghost in general.

Amelia, a former waitress, was standing in the front part of the café cleaning up. Out of the corner of her eye, she caught a glimpse of a shadow figure in the very back storage room moving from east to west. Amelia thought it might be a vendor or one of the other employees. Calling out, she received no response. Amelia walked to the back of the building, only to find herself alone.

When we investigated the restaurant, we did it during normal business hours as the family went about their normal business. While we talked about the figure in the back room, we caught the shadow on film. All of us were astounded.

Several times throughout the year, the deep fryer clicks on and off. Although it's been checked and it seems in perfect working order,

Photos taken in the back room of Marlows. Notice the black shadow gaining size and darkness on the right side of the photos.

the Marlow's say they consider it someone "talking to us" when it happens. Many times occurrences happen and they are blamed on ghosts. Annette says, "That's my story and I'm sticking to it!" Lights in the kitchen seem to mirror the deep fryer issues, going out at curious times. Pots and pans will fall off racks. Additionally, the front "Open" sign will be turned off, only to be back on in the morning. Sometimes the sign doesn't wait that long to come back on. One day at closing time, the light was turned off by Courtney, a long-time server. Sarah, another server said, "Don't forget to turn off the light!" Courtney looked over at it and said, "I know I turned that off!" Annette echoed the statement, as she saw Courtney do it.

But, that's not where it all ended. Annette has had other paranormal events occur in the building. As we stood next to the grill during my interview, she turned to me and said, "See how I can see myself in the windows across the street? Many mornings, when I look at the windows, I have someone in white standing with me. When I turn to see who it is, I find no one."

When I brought in a copy of this story to fact check, Michael and I stopped to have breakfast. As Annette answered some last-minute questions, Kate, a newer waitress asked, "Should anything be smoking?"

Annette's eyes grew wide, "What? What do you mean? What is smoking?"

When they went to the kitchen together, they found the grill turned up on high. Apparently, we've "riled up" the spirits. I choose to think they are excited about the story.

In the morning hours in Westfield, any number of locals are seen in the café. From parents with young children to older men talking about the past, the café has always been a mainstay– a staple of the community. Today, suburbanites up for a substantial meal before starting lawn work also patronize the business. The Marlows are happy to serve all their customers.

Even the Marlows who may have left the earth years ago.

The Marlows enjoy cooking for their customers. The owners take great pride in the quality of their food and service. (L to r. Lindsay, Annette, and Bob)

MILL CREEK ROAD

Corner of State Road 32 and Mill Creek Road

The last thing on Robert Paskiet's mind that early October morning a little after 4 a.m. was dying. As he whipped through fog-shrouded State Road 32, little did he know he'd end up dead with a broken neck and fractured skull- and at the hand, or truck in this case, of his neighbor, John L. Waak of Westfield. Before all was said and done, Robert lost control of his motorcycle and was smashed into by John, who flipped him onto the hood of his truck and traveled 90 feet before stopping.

Not much is known about Robert. He was born on February 21, 1944 to William and Dorothy Paskiet and was married to Sandra Axell on April 18, 1964. He worked in Indianapolis as a book binder at Bookwalters and he was a member of the Fish Lake Mennonite Church. At the time of his death, Robert had three living daughters (another daughter died early in life), three brothers and three sisters. He was buried at Pine Lake Cemetery in LaPorte.

Mill Creek Road is another story. At one time Mill Creek Road and State Road 32 was Model Mill land. The Model Mill was a mill that was not only functional but also showed other mills how their mills could operate using the machinery at the Model Mill. The land stretched from State Road 32 down Mill Creek Road and across to State Road 38. The Model Mill started out as the Noblesville Milling Company located in Noblesville and grew its own crops to make into flour (as well as vegetables). As the Model Mill branched out into creating products for the Indiana Baking Company, Indiana Donuts and McMahon Industries (also food related), the need for this wheat was great. The building also housed the Indiana Seed Company for a time. Today, the mill building now houses various businesses and a conference center and is also haunted.

Paskiet's unfortunate death was not the only one at this location – oh no. In 1931 Robert King was killed by one of his friends by joyriding in a convertible one early evening east on State Road 32 toward Noblesville, near the same intersection. King's friend, Revere Cox was showing off his "Pontiac coach". First he headed west then turned around and headed back east when he lost control of his car. It ran off the road and flipped several times. Robert's friends were able to pull him from the wreckage. All the kids (2 boys and 2 girls) were taken to the hospital. Robert lingered until 10 p.m. He never regained consciousness and according to his distraught friends, some of whom were also hospitalized, they later saw him walking the corridors of the hospital at night. He was only 15.

The hospital isn't the only place that one of these ghosts is seen. While the terrain of the area has changed, it seems the people who have passed through it have not. State Road 32 between Westfield and Noblesville used to be a series of homesteads broken up by the occasional business. Over the last 15 years, the land has been gobbled up by housing and commercial districts and the once flat, straight 5 minute drive to Noblesville, has now become a 15 minute stop-light fest.

Most of the old Model Mill farm is dotted with homes, and a housing addition named for the mill now sits on a large chunk of the land. At the corner of State Road 32 and Mill Creek Road now stands a small used car dealership and an empty Ritter's frozen custard stand on the northeast side of the highway.

However, one thing hasn't changed. Despite the area's growth, the stretch of road where the accidents occurred collects thick fog during late evening hours and the fogs sometimes last well past noon the next day. It is precisely on those evenings that the sound of impact is heard and cadaverous figures appear.

One couple I spoke with described their full-color experience. They work at a local hospital on the same shift and are very familiar with the stretch of road. "We know how dangerous the road can get. When we came home that evening, we were trying to be extra careful with the fog." Jenny paused, "It was so thick, we couldn't see more than past our own car. As we drove down the road, right past Mill Creek [Road], we heard the most horrendous skidding, as if on wet pavement and a thump, like something soft hitting the pavement, you know," Jenny trailed off.

Exactly like someone flying off a motorcycle.

"We pulled over and stopped the car. Jared and I just looked at each other. We couldn't see anything. No other cars were out. Both of us stepped out of the car and stood in front of it. It was off, but the lights were still on. Then we heard it. The worst wailing in the world." Jenny's large blue eyes were saddened at the thought. "We wanted to do something, you know, but we couldn't see anybody or anything.

Jared grabbed a flashlight from the trunk and went down the road a ways."

At this point in the interview, Jenny looked at Jared and asked if he wanted to talk about what happened next. Reluctantly, he spoke in a halting voice. "I got down the road just about a hundred feet or so and I saw a truck and a motorcycle. It wasn't pretty. It looked like the truck hit the bike and dragged it for a while." Jared looked directly at me. "The guy on the bike was messed up pretty bad. The guy in the truck was slumped over the wheel, but I could hear someone right there, screaming. Just yelling. " Jared took a deep breath. "I knew we needed to get some help, but I wanted to see what we were dealing with. I started to walk over to them and they were gone. Just gone. I've never experienced anything like it."

Jenny explained, "I remember when the wailing stopped. The next thing I knew Jared was running back and getting into the car. He was absolutely shaken up. I got in too and I was asking him what happened. He didn't want to talk about it. The only thing he said was 'I don't believe it.' As we drove through where he came from, Jared slowed down and looked out the window. But found nothing."

"I asked at the hospital the next day if anyone was brought in from an accident – no one was going to forget that kind of damage to someone –but no one had been brought in. " Jared took a deep breath. "To this day, I don't understand how we can hear this accident, and I see it. And it disappeared."

What Jenny and Jared experienced could very well have been a residual haunting of the accident. Because of the intense and violent nature of the accident, the organic footprint of the event could be imprinted in the area. People who believe in residual haunting generally believe that the event plays over and over like a movie with no contact made between the people in the event and the living that see the interaction. More recently, paranormal investigators are rethinking this idea. More modern theories suggest the very idea that the living are able to see or hear the event classifies it as making contact or an acknowledgement from the dead to the living –an intelligent haunting. This is different from the intelligent hauntings in which the spirits interact with you, even talk with you. But intelligent nonetheless.

Jenny and Jared were not the only people to see something unearthly on this road. In retrospect, Susan Peterson and Harold Knox think maybe they had their experience because they were in close age to Robert King and his friends. The couple was dating and had taken a weekend trip to visit some of Susan's family. On the way home, they got the surprise of their lives when they saw a young woman on their side of the road walking towards Noblesville.

The night was fair and warm, but when the couple pulled over to see if they could help the girl, they both felt chilled. The young woman looked as if she'd been "beat up and dragged through the bushes. Her face had several abrasions and she was holding her arm as if it were broken. She wore a hat that was half off her head and her hair was escaping its careful pinning. Susan noticed the girl's light blouse had blood on it.

Susan asked the girl how they could help. The girl said her friends had been in a car accident and she needed to get help. Harry got out and opened the door, helping the woman inside. He asked the woman where her friends were and she said back down the road a little ways. Although neither Susan nor Harry had seen anything on the road, they went back, "in case the car was off in a ditch", explained Susan. Harry drove slowly in the increasing night trying to find where they went off. Susan turned around to the girl and asked where exactly they had the accident. The girl, according to Susan, looked confused and shook her head saying, "Rob's dead." She put her head in her hands and wept. As Susan reached to comfort the girl, the girl disappeared.

"I was absolutely silent. Harry looked over and asked what the problem was. He said I was ashen." Susan reminisced, "I told him that she was gone. He told me I was nuts and when he turned to look, he saw he was nuts too."

The pair mused over the incident all the way home, trying to "rationalize it". They had no other choice but to conclude it was paranormal.

It is interesting to note that if this was one of Robert King's friends, she must have been thinking what she was saying. Neither girl involved in the accident was seriously hurt, and Robert didn't die until he got to the hospital. But thinking about this even further, Robert King was never conscious after the accident. What if he had a conversation with his friends after the wreck, as a ghost? This would explain why none of them were eager to speak to the authorities. (True, Cox would be reluctant because he could have been charged with involuntary manslaughter). What if this conversation took place and one of the girls tried walking back to Noblesville to get help. With such an emotional scene, for people who believe in residual hauntings, this is not a great leap. A residual haunting is the organic imprint of events and emotions at a location. There was certainly both that night in 1931.

Whether residual or intelligent hauntings, the tragic accidents that have happened on this stretch of road left an impression not only on the victims' families but also in those who have seen the victims long after their deaths.

The mill's farm land is now nothing more than a memory commemorated in the names of Mill Farm Road and Drive. The land that once was covered with wheat and other grains is now dotted with large homes and ample grounds for families to relax. Mill Creek Road still fogs up badly from time to time. Because of the way the landscape has been shaped by progress, in the late winter, snow lingers on the south side of the road, pouring fog across it. Just as it did that October night.

State Road 32 and Mill Creek Road: The scene of a fatal accident and ghostly apparitions.

SLEEPY HOLLOW

East Side of North Union Street; north of Old Town Hall

Westfield is certainly no setting for Ichabod Crane or the Headless Horseman to make his nightly ride, but it does have a section in the middle of town that is haunted nonetheless. From earliest times, this grove of trees was a common area for friends to gather and the town to meet. Situated behind the old town hall, which was the Congressional Church, many times on a Sunday, people would host picnics in this spot. The children would play games and the older folks would sit and talk about different times. The women would take time to get caught up on family news- births, deaths and other happenings. The men would swap news of planting, harvesting, and politics.

The area changed hands over the years and is currently owned by the Christ Methodist Church. It still stands as a wooded grove that was nicknamed "Sleepy Hollow" as it is as drowsy, enchanted, and bewitching as Washington Irving's Sleepy Hollow was described in 1820. By day it is an innocent, beckoning area of respite.

By night, the beckoning is for something quite different.

The shadows of the trees seem to close in oppressively to some. Others cannot bear to be in the area for longer than a couple of minutes. Some visitors swear they've had conversations with some of the early settlers.

Sara Stuart was just one of these people. While visiting relatives, she had a lot of opportunity to explore Westfield. She'd talked with some of her family's neighbors about the beauty of Westfield and Hamilton County. A little neighbor girl piped up and told her, "You don't want to go over there after dark." pointing to Sleepy Hollow. When pressed, the girl gravely told her, "It's haunted. They'll get you."

Of course, Sara wanted to check it out. "I was sure it was just an overactive child's imagination." Sara and a girlfriend sat out in the tall trees and waited, but experienced nothing. During her visit, she came back a few more times. Finally, she went alone on the night before she was to return home. "It was dark in the trees. The section toward the church was the darkest of all. I sat there, watching the streetlights on Union and Penn Streets. The area was quiet despite the houses around. I looked through the trees and thought I saw shadows shifting through the trees to the south of me. I got up to take a look, thinking it was most likely just the leaves and branches from adjoining trees. As I moved towards the shadows, I realized there seemed to be more- thicker. By the time I'd reached the edge of the trees, they were around me. An army of shadow figures with no faces but in the general shape of a human."

She paused in her story, eyes looking back on the memory. "It was like time was suspended. There was only the dark, and these dark shadows. They weren't talking- at least I couldn't see them talking, but I could hear them speaking. They all wanted to tell me their stories. Children, men, women. All of them wanted to talk to me. They were friendly and came from all walks of life. There was a grocer who lost his wife in childbirth who missed her very much. There was a former slave from Louisiana who was helped by some families and stayed in the area. And one child I remember said she died of a fever and missed her favorite doll. I felt very wanted; it was almost overwhelming. Cloying. They came closer and I heard myself cry out from the feeling of being pressed in on."

Sara blinked, clearing her mind, and sighed. "The next thing I knew, I was being picked up off the ground by my cousin." She laughed, "My cousin couldn't believe the tale, but the neighbor girl did. 'I told you they'd get you.' You know," Sara's voice trailed off, "I kind of believe her now too."

Sara's story was fantastic to believe but I had no reason to dis-believe her. I tend to take everything with a grain of salt. Over time, we've had people, even pseudo paranormal investigators try to tell us stories that were falsified, for whatever reason. However, in the years it's taken to write this book, I now can believe Sara's story wholeheart-edly. During some of our private tours, we've taken guests to Sleepy Hollow and let them experiment with ghost hunting equipment, includ-ing digital voice recorders, cameras and even dowsing rods.

Dowsing or divining was done as early as the 1400s and may have originated in Germany. Called *Glueck Ruet* (fortune rods/sticks), they were used to find water, minerals and metals. They were usually cut from wood. Willow was preferred and made into a "Y" shape. The user held the top part of the "Y" and the single branch was held forth to find what one sought. Today, "L"-shaped metal rods represent the willow wood most often. Although many people believe this to be bunk, dowsing rods have been very accurate in finding water, graves and even grave stones. In the paranormal world, people use them to speak with the dead. When the rods cross, it is an affirmative answer. When they don't cross, it is a negative answer.

With use of the dowsing rods, many tour guests and investigators have found a variety of people who want to speak. Invariably these people claim to be residents of Westfield. Nowhere in over 30 years of paranormal investigation have I found a place so full of unrelated people who have been eager to talk (not even in locations such as hospitals). With each investigation however, the communication seems to be jammed in some way. Or perhaps there are simply too many people clamoring for attention. Investigators from Indiana and out of state have suggested that perhaps because of the history of Westfield, that the town was tight-knit enough to want to stay together in death. Some investigators believe whole-heartedly that the spirits need to be sent on. I believe the truth lies somewhere between and that the spirits of Sleepy Hollow mean no harm. Rather they want to make sure that they are not forgotten. And who can blame them?

Visitors report phantom shadows and conversations with the dead in this seemingly quiet grove of trees.

OLD FIRE STATION

145 South Union Street

As the boy watched the block burn, he thought the flames reaching higher into the night sky looked like the hands of God, ready to strike down that which was impure. And why not? His dad told him that smoking was bad and here was the pipe store up in flames. He watched the fire department hose the flames from the Model T fire truck, but it didn't seem to do any good. A shiver ran down his spine. What he wouldn't give to be one of those firemen working on taming the fire that had spread over three buildings. The boy turned his eyes to the shoe shop owner who was shaking his head, and to the man's wife who was clutching a handkerchief in her hands. The yellow gold flames danced in the wet tears on her face.

This fire was a good one, but it was smaller in comparison with the other fires his father and those on the bucket brigade who had fought it talked about. The fire of 1915 had burnt a whole lumberyard. In 1904 the public school in town burned (too bad they rebuilt it!). But the fire of 1898, as it was called, burned the same block. During the first fire, a drug store, a grocer, a dry goods store, a newspaper office, the only bank in town at the time and the library burned to the ground. To hear the stories told, the embers from the fire stayed hot and smoky for over two days.

Robert Mikesell turned his face back to the fire that was destroying his old school. He watched the school as it was built in 1925 and later attended it as a teenager. So many memories wrapped up in the school. Robert had been around enough fires to know this one would make the school a total loss and the school would most likely be razed.

Later, as the firemen put their equipment away, the mood was somber. Thankfully, no one had been killed, but the fire was still a huge blow to the community. The high school was a place of meeting for the town and it seemed as if with the passing of the building, a piece of each of the firemen went with it.

The fire department was established in Westfield around 1904. Although the fire department had a 1904 Boyer Fire Cart and other

Westfield Fire Department 1967. Front row, left to right: Harold Mikesell, Art Baldwin, Andy Tracy, Bob Stiepp, Buck Talbott, Bob Edwards. Back row, left to right: V.J. "Bit" Macy, Elmer Spelbring, Bob Mikesell, Earl Watkins.

(Photo courtesy of the Westfield Washington Historical Society)

equipment to fight fires, they rented a garage in which they kept the equipment. In 1923 approval was given to build an engine house, town hall and comfort station (rest rooms) for about $2,000. The firehouse was built on South Union Street, about a block from State Road 32. It is a Mission -style brick building, with a covered porch with plenty of large windows to let in healthy sunlight. Beside it were other commercial buildings (before New Jersey Street was built).

Today, the fire station is home to the Westfield Washington Historical Society and Museum and Open Doors, an organization sponsored by 15 churches, which is dedicated to helping people in need of food, clothing and other services. Many people visit the building on a regular basis from clients to museum visitors, volunteers and staff for both organizations. One person remains a constant. Robert "Bob" Mikesell, born October 9, 1918 and died on August 7, 2005. He was a Westfield firefighter and Fire Chief for many years. By all accounts he was very well respected, from an earlier family who had settled in the community – and as crazy as the stereotypical firefighter.

At the time the museum was in the process of opening I was the Communications Officer for the historical society. Several officers knew something was not right with the building. When we'd gone to inspect it to see if we could even use the building, three of us had an experience. The officers had started to walk up the stairs to the area that we would occupy. Two women were in front of me and I was hanging back a bit looking in some old filing cabinets for some history. I felt a definite wind rush by me. Before I could react, the two women, one after the other asked if I had felt a breeze blow by. While one woman was immediately apprehensive and the other was curious. I was thoroughly delighted.

During this time, I was working in consulting and had decided to donate a large chunk of time to helping make this community dream a reality. I wrote a grant which secured a $35,000 grant for the project, I spent quite a bit of time in the building and as all buildings do it displayed a cacophony of noise, bumps and pops throughout the days and nights. What I couldn't let go of were the footsteps down the stairs, which seemed to continue down the last few stairs we dismantled. Nor could I quite let go of voices calling my name when I was the only person in the building.

The first time these occurrences began, it was early summer. Members had been collecting items for the museum for years, myself included. With the announcement that a museum would be created, people from Westfield and beyond had generously donated items to the historical society. I dug into creating a time line and a schedule for tasks to be completed before the museum opened. The best part of my tasks was researching and creating the displays. I consulted with other museums and exhibit creators and put together a plan for these tasks to be completed as well. As part of the research, I needed to sort through the items to be accessioned into the collection before I could use them. Many days I sorted through and took pictures of items and a teenager came in part time to do the actual accessioning, data entry and tagging.

On this day, however, she was not in and I was busy sorting so that when she returned, she would have a lot of items waiting for her to process. I set up my workspace in the main room (what was part of engine room) on two huge tables and began to take pictures of the precious items. To the back of me was the upper newer rest room and the doorway that led upstairs (to the right) and what used to lead downstairs to the basement (to the left). For security and insurance purposes, the stairs that continued downward had been removed and the old comfort station rest rooms had been repaired and reopened for the organization downstairs.

As I continued to work, I heard a scrape upstairs but thought nothing of it. To me, it could have been one of the many items upstairs shifting, as we had yet to put complete order to any of the items in the museum. I continued working intently, enjoying my task and zoning out. Some time later, I became aware of a measured walk down the stairs. I was mildly interested as I knew I was the only person in the building. Still, I thought perhaps one of the other members was working on the air conditioning and had come up the roof in the back and in through the roof door. I turned, half expecting to see the historical society president, but my eyes saw nothing human. I listened but heard no more.

I went back to work zoning out again and a few minutes later, I heard footsteps again. This time, they were coming from where the stairs had been removed and continued right up to the second floor. My paranormal instincts kicked in and I went up the stairs, camera in hand, snapping pictures and taking video. I asked if anyone was there and received silence. The upstairs was a maze of boxes, furniture and accessioning supplies. After a thorough search of the area, including the old firemens' rest rooms, shower and locker room areas, I concluded that no living person was in the building with me. I told whoever it was that they needed to make the best of the situation and that the historical society was moving in and preserving the town's history as well as it could. My investigation revealed no unusual evidence- not even an orb.

A week or so later, I heard my name called from upstairs. It had been another week of the same tasks. People in the community were becoming almost frantic to have the historical society open and some people had a hidden agenda for accomplishing this task. Many politically driven meetings had taken place and as a result, we were losing volunteers. When I heard my name, I called back, "What can I do for you?" The footsteps started down the stairs. Thoroughly creeped out, hair standing on my arms, I approached the doorway and waited for something, anything to appear. Still nothing.

I mentioned the happenings to some of volunteers and officers of the historical society. People expressed reactions ranging from nervous laughter and disbelief to curiosity. One member quipped, "Maybe it's Bob." They showed me a picture of Bob Mikesell, who had passed away just a year before. "Maybe." I stated noncommittally.

A little later in summer, I needed to get back to my clients – business was good. During my stay at the historical society, I'd tried EVP work, taking pictures, video, even automatic writing and dowsing rods, but nothing concrete came from any of the efforts. The construction was done, the air conditioner fixed, and the museum was almost open. My efforts had paid off and I was proud of what I'd accomplished.

It wasn't too long after I had disengaged myself from the museum somewhat that Michael, who was vice president of the historical society at the time (now Curator), brought home more tales. The same phenomenon I'd experienced had now been experienced by other members and volunteers. Once, when they were discussing Bob a clock fell off the wall. It had been securely fastened with toggle bolts and the hook on the clock lay inside a lipped groove. Everyone agreed it was highly unlikely it could have fallen without extra help. That same afternoon, a volunteer was working on an exhibit and put out some pictures in the upstairs area that used to be the kitchen. She went downstairs to ask someone a question. When she returned, the pictures had been scattered over the floor, although no windows were open. Later, we discovered it was Bob Mikesell's death anniversary.

The museum exudes a great spirit of community energy. I hope Bob and any other spirits in the building feel the same way.

Stairway in the old firestation where people report hearing footsteps while working and visiting.

The old firestation as it looks today. The Westfield Washington (Township) Historical Society is in the oldest part of the building. Open Doors utilizes the newer bays on the southwest side of the building.

The old fire station when it was practically brand new. The building used to have a covered porch area. Can you see the cat curled up on the porch post? The man in the foreground is helping pave Union Street. Also note to the south of the fire station is another building. It was torn down to make room for New Jersey Street!

(Photo courtesy of the Westfield Washington Historical Society)

FOOD AND SPIRITS

102-108 South Union Street

In 1889, Bob Funderburgh and his father Arthur opened Funderburgh & Sons Grocers at 104 North Union Street (now Hobson Insurance). Later, they moved to 102 South Union Street. They were known for a sanitary store that carried high quality products and made home deliveries. A "sanitary store" meant that it was clean and followed health requirements. In the 1880s the State Board of Health was founded and started making and enforcing food and drink purity laws. They also enforced laws pertaining to the condition of buildings, especially ones that dealt in foodstuffs.

In the 1930s, the store closed and the location became a diner and in 1958 Pickett's Cafeteria. Bernard "Bernie" and Mary Pickett bought the restaurant and started serving their delicious food from one salad table, one steam table and a grill. The food was homemade, with Mary making cream and meringue pies and the sides. Bernie made the fruit pies and the meats. On a Sunday, it was not unusual to serve up to 600 people a day. Their meals were legendary, the most famous of which was the fried chicken. In 1972 the Pickett's sold the business but it continued to run as Pickett's Cafeteria for years.

Cliff Bradley bought the property and ran it as a cafeteria for many years. The business was fine, however, odd occurrences started to happen when Cliff was remodeling the kitchen and cleaned out an old flue pipe. He found and removed an old hooch crock, which sat in the restaurant as decoration for quite a while. Cliff once said that customers remember seeing the apparition of a woman and a little girl in turn of the century clothing. Although no documented records have uncovered any tragedy such as a murder, the stories persist. Additionally, Cliff and his staff would find food missing and kitchen equipment moved, but all staff members denied being a part of the activities. They began to blame these occurrences on Bernie.

Later, Jan's Village Pizza rented the buildings and had a spin-off restaurant, Jan's Italian Village. When Michael and I were asked to be on Fox 59 in 2003, we knew exactly where we needed to be. We arrived at 5:30 in the morning and decided how we'd set up the equipment and where we wanted to shoot. Originally, the basement of the

Jan's Village Pizza today. At one time the building had three stories. To the far left is the original outside entrance to the upper floors. Maybe on your next visit you'll be greeted by Bernie!

Italian Village was the focus. Not only did it have a tunnel, believed to be part of the Underground Railroad, but employees reported sightings of shadow figures.

We waited for the crew to show up and began talking about some of the things that had been happening. The lights had been flickering off and on, although an electrician could find no reason for it. Additionally, when the lights would flicker invariably we would show up, as if something was waiting for us. Other paranormal happenings included:

- Employees had a general sense of being watched.
- Many times when the section between the 102 and 104 building was closed because it wasn't needed or because it was late in the evening, waitresses and other staff would hear their names called from this area. Ironically, this is the same area in which the hooch crock from the chimney flue was displayed.
- The teenage girls who were employed at the time report having had someone blow on their necks while in the kitchen area of both restaurants and in the serving area of the Italian Village.
- The same people would feel someone run a hand down their arms while vacuuming the middle section.
- Many times food would be found missing. On one particular occasion, lasagna went missing. The next day, the pan was found put back in its washed and put away!
- Footsteps were heard overhead (even in Jan's Village Pizza, which hasn't had a second or third story for decades!)

Garry Brush, the manager and Jan Miller, co-owner, mentioned the upper floor over the Italian Village section and how creepy it was. We decided that the three of us would go up. Michael would wait for the television crew.

We made our way up outside and opened the coarse wooden door. Although it's been replaced, it was a plank door with a board at the top and bottom to hold it together. A simple padlock served as security. We proceeded up the wooden stairs that had indeed seen better days and turned the corner to enter the rough upstairs section of the old Picket's cafeteria.

From the time Michael and I moved in, not only had we heard

that location was part of the Underground Railroad, but that at one time, the upstairs had been a brothel. People in Westfield are not inclined to talk about this rumor. After all it is a town founded by Quakers and they did not like secrets or secret societies, so the general consensus of people who have lived there forever is that there was no such place. But other people in town tend to think more progressively. After all, although the town was founded on Quaker principles, other religions and people lived in the town. True, there was no alcohol until the first short-lived saloon, which was no more than a couple barrels and a wooden plank. It was built on the railroad right-of-way and cut to ribbons by women (and men) who were of the temperance movement. Still, there had to be people with human urges, especially railroad men. After all, no one is perfect.

As we stepped into the dark area, we could see bits of light from street lamps coming through the eaves. Our eyes adjusted and we were told there was no electricity upstairs, so feeling in the dark with the aid of a flashlight, we made our way through. There was just one narrow corridor with rooms on either side which could suggest the rumors were correct- very conducive to privacy and getting a lot of rooms in for very common business.

The morning was unseasonably warm for Halloween Day and there was a good stiff warm breeze blowing. However, the area had an undercurrent of cold. Garry was the first to comment on it. We ventured into each small room. Most rooms were stripped down to studs and held unused restaurant and seasonal equipment. We started with our EMF detector and pictures. Unusual spikes happened in a couple of the rooms and the temperature started to drop. Jan sat the fence on the paranormal, said she felt ill and needed to leave. Shortly after that Garry said he felt the same way. I stayed upstairs for a few more minutes and then felt ill as well. We all agreed that when we'd made it downstairs, we immediately felt better.

When the crew arrived and caught wind that we'd had some interesting experiences upstairs, we immediately decided to do some of the filming there. The interviews went wonderfully and electricity and excitement were in the air. I spoke quite a bit between segments with the camera woman, who believed her own apartment was haunted. She'd found her front door open several times and heard the click of the door without it opening several times.

As we finished filming the last segment upstairs, we demon-

Michael Kobrowski (l.) and Garry Brush (r.) investigate the upper floor of the building at the southeast corner or Union Street and State Road 32. Several orbs are present. Michael also reported spikes in the EMF meter although no electrical sources were present.

strated our equipment and took some pictures. Within minutes, we had people on the phone telling us to check our film as there was an orb that followed my husband as he went around the room during the demonstration. Sure enough, when we looked back through the film, a bright white orb darted around him.

We went back into Jan's while the camera woman gathered her cables. She seemed to be taking a long time so I went to see what I could do to help her. She was standing at the outside door pulling on the cords that were still upstairs. "I'm not going up there and you can't make me," she declared adamantly. I asked what was wrong and she indicated that she was in the doorway trying to pull the cords and the plank door swung and hit her with full force.

Despite the wind, this was impossible. The door was old and held to the frame by three hinges. These hinges were old and drooping. To open the door all the way, one had to unlock it, pull it forward and then lift up on it and carry it back. Otherwise, it dragged the sidewalk (for a long time, there was an arch on the sidewalk where it was dragged). However, the wind was no more than 10 miles per hour.

The camerawoman felt that there was something up there that did not like her because she had been talking about the ghost in her apartment. I went back and got Michael and the others and we helped her get the cables and equipment in order.

But this wasn't to be the end. These mysterious events continue to this day- more or less. Jan has gone back to just her pizza parlor and Queso Blanco, some of the finest Mexican food in Indiana, has opened in the 102 building. The lights still flicker, and the upstairs, despite some remodeling, retains the uneasy feeling.

Additionally, several member of one of our tours saw a young boy looking out the top most window of Queso Blanco. We asked the staff if anyone was upstairs and they indicated it was empty. There was no way that a boy could have been in that window at the angle he was for a couple reasons. First, he would have had to have been on a ladder, as it was a good 12 feet off the ground. Second, he was in front of a curtain and when he moved away, he moved through the curtain.

The owner of Queso Blanco believes in the paranormal, but he wants to leave it alone. A table was removed from the restaurant after several people saw it levitate. It was returned months later. Some people say a device had been installed on it to make it do this. Others believe it was paranormal. Time will tell.

The Jan from Jan's Village Pizza. Her award-winning pizza is worth the trip!

The old Pickett's Cafeteria, now home to Queso Blanco. Missing food, feelings of sickness, a ghostly child and many more paranormal treats lurk in this building.

STATE BANK OF WESTFIELD

100 North Union Street

When Michael and I were called into the former State Bank of Westfield, we were not expecting the treat that came out of our visits.

The bank was organized in March of 1884 by several members of Westfield's early families, including Lewis Estes, Elim Conklin, Robert Estes, J.N. Parr and Abel Doan. The original red brick building was on the west side of South Union Street (where the Westfield Pharmacy Parking lot currently stands). It burned in 1898 and the next year, the new bank was built in its current location. The land where this bank sits is considered to be part of the Underground Railroad, as there is a tunnel that runs between this building and the building across State Road 32 (currently Queso Blanco). The bank was burglarized only once in 1911 when safecrackers robbed the bank. During the bank panic of 1929-1930, the bank closed but reopened under the name, Union State Bank. The original vault is still in the basement and is used for storage.

Since the bank closed sometime after 1984, the building has been a series of hair salons, bridal stores, art studios, gift shops, a mortgage company, Pilates studio, and recently, a photography business. When it was a bank, ornate metal and wood teller cages dominated the downstairs. When we were brought in to investigate, the dominating feature was the stairway to the upper level, which had been added late in the building's history. A desk and long conference table were the only items downstairs. Upstairs, desks ringed the donut-shaped area. Harold* took me to his desk on the upper floor.

His desk had been hit by a tornado, or so I thought. His computer and monitor were scattered on the floor, still connected and running, oddly enough. Papers dotted the desk and chair haphazardly. I asked him what happened, to which Harold replied, "It had to be a ghost." I thought maybe someone had broken in and asked if that might not be a possibility. He adamantly shook his head no. "Look at my plants." And indeed, dust had gathered and remained on each of them. So no one could have come in his window. The other window sills were in similar condition, minus the plants.

I went back downstairs with Harold and asked everyone what had been going on. The owner, Jeri* stated, "The only reason you're here is because it's costing me money. I tell my employees to bring in a sweater and I keep it pretty cool in here in the winter." Her employees nodded, almost in unison. Jeri continued, "We've come in on several occasions and the heat has been turned up to 90 degrees. At first, I thought my employees were responsible but I know now that they aren't."

I listened carefully and asked if anything else had been happening. Jeri tutted, "I used to have an employee who was Wiccan and he said he'd seen a woman and a little girl in here on the stairs."

The information wasn't blowing my skirt up and I sensed there was something else. "What else has been happening?" I asked.

The group looked from one to the other and finally, Jeri said simply, "All of us have seen a man in bib overalls looking down at us from the top of the stairs."

Now this was something to ponder. No one had any contact or conversations with any of the entities, yet, something may have contacted them through Harold's desk and the constant watching. As always, I asked the group what they wanted to get out of this. Did they want to live with it, get rid of it or something else?

Harold spoke up and said, "I think we all want to know who it is and why the things are happening."

I nodded and asked to go upstairs to take some pictures and do some EVP work. The group needed to get back to work, so I was flying solo. I walked the upper area and stairs asking questions and explaining who the people were and what they were doing in the building. When I'd finished, I told the group I'd pull the history on the building and do some other checking and get back with them.

When I examined the photos and the recorder, I wasn't surprised that I didn't capture anything. I am a firm believer in involving the people who are experiencing the phenomenon. Unfortunately in this case, they had to get back to work. I went to the historical society and pulled what we knew about the bank. While I was there, I asked the president if he knew anything about the bank. Jim had lived in Westfield the majority of his life and was a wealth of historical information. When I mentioned that there was a man in bib overalls seen in the bank, Jim, who sits the fence a bit about the paranormal, laughed and said, "That must be ol' Hank West." I asked who he was and if we had a picture. Jim pointed me in the right direction and told me he was the unofficial night watchman of the bank.

Regardless of media hype, you don't always get something on film or via digital voice recorder. You don't always get the history to line up with the events either, although 9 times out of 10 you can make a connection. I looked at Hank's photo. Even as an older gentleman he still looked handsome and very much alive. Although the picture was in black and white, he seemed to have a little mischievousness in his look. I decided to take three photos back to the business with me. Three photos of men in bib overalls.

I gave the history to the group and then told them I had a question for each of them. I brought them to the table individually and asked if any of the people in the pictures looked familiar. Every person picked Hank West.

Frank "Hank" West was far more than just an unofficial night watchman of a bank. His story started in the east as a one of many children who came to Indiana through the Orphan Train Movement. Over 200,000 children went through this process although many of them were not orphans. In addition to orphans, children whose parents could not afford to feed them and those children who were simply unwanted, were also dropped off. They were placed by the Children's Aid Society. Many times the children did not know what was going to happen to them. Older children were excited for the trip and adventure.

For some children, new parents were waiting. Local agencies would try to make sure local families were fit to accept children but the checks are not like today's adoption process. Some children were separated from their siblings. Other children couldn't be placed and would be put in local orphan homes, which was the case with Hank West. These children sometimes had marginally better lives than living on the streets or in poverty. Other times, the children were just as bad off, having been adopted by people who treated them no better than slaves. This does not seem to be the case with Hank.

From the history we know, the Westfield Orphanage, also known as the Indiana Receiving Home at Westfield, was a clean, well maintained location, run for most of its approximately six years by Calvin and Rose Carey and later by Reverend F.M. Elliot of Indianapolis. The children cared for in Westfield, were treated the same as any other children. They were well dressed, well-fed and went to public schools. Chores consisted of labor children would have to perform anyway-dishes, feeding chickens, etc.

Hank lived in the home until he was about 16. At that time, it is

The Old Westfield Bank. Built in 1898, it is still inhabited by Hank West, who is still on the job, caring for the building.

not clear what he did as a profession. The orphan home always dis-charged grown children with gainful employment. We do know that he served as a private in the US Army during WWI and he was the unof-ficial night watchman at the bank. Later in life, Hank was the Westfield Town Marshall for a time. He also "served" with the firefighters in West-field.

Once, the firemen were sent to fight a fire close to Joiletville. Hank jumped on the back of the truck as it took off. As they rattled down the road, a severe thunderstorm hit the group and large chunks of hail beat down upon them. When they got to the burning building that night, Hank was carrying about 20 pounds of ice inside his shirt and he was frozen from the ride over. The firemen, so it is said, let him warm up first by the fire before they put it out.

For Harold and his coworkers, perhaps Hank was ever on the watch, ensuring the bank was safe, although it was no longer there. He could have also been confused about the whole layout and wondered where the bank was after all these years. I related my stories about Hank and his past to the group. I told them one last thing. A woman with whom I spoke about Hank but not about the haunting told me that Hank used to make his landlord, Camilla Axelrod, very upset. I asked her why and she said, "He used to turn the heat up so high, her electric bill would skyrocket."

The room was silent. I asked again what they wanted from it. They all said they just wanted him not to scare them anymore, and to stop playing with the heat.

I told the group they had to take charge of the situation and let Hank know that it wasn't ok to move the thermostat. From that time on, to my knowledge, they never had any more issues with Hank.

However, that wasn't to be the end of the story. Other tenants have reported strange feelings in the building as if they were being watched. For Lindsey Berry owner of Perfect Pilates Studio, it became more.

Shortly after she moved in to the building, Lindsey had several episodes where her hair stood up on her body and she felt the pres-ence of someone. Additionally, her alarm system was set up to beep when someone would come in, but it beeped at random times when she was by herself. Often over the 18 months she rented the building, Lindsey was upstairs with clients and they would hear someone come in the door. When they called down to them, no one would answer, and no one would be in the building. Finally, before she moved, Lindsey said her husband thought she was "crazy" because she thought at night she heard a child crying. In fact, the sound was so prevalent, Lindsey stopped having evening classes because of it. "I was scared," she explained. She's never had another problem.

While interviewing Lindsey, I asked if she'd ever had heating or air conditioning issues. She said she did have a thermostat issue. For her, the thermostat would be turned way up high or down really low. Much like Jeri, she also thought her instructors were changing the thermostat and because of it, she installed locks on them. She came in one day and the lock had been removed as though someone had tried to hit it with something heavy. Her father in law said someone had tried to take it off. At first, Lindsey thought one of her Pilates balls had hit it, but could find no evidence of it. After that, she put a heavy duty lock on it.

Lindsey also relayed the story of the ghost of a little boy. When it was a bank, a little boy whose father had a business down the street would come to visit. Apparently, there was an accident at the bank and the boy died.

The bank is an active place to be sure, and as we've continued to investigate it over the years, we've found that while it was under the ownership of different businesses, these people also experienced strange phenomenon, including lights turning off and on, doors banging, and shadow figures rushing up the basement stairs.

Although we don't know at the present who the boy might be or when this accident occurred or even who or what has caused the ruckus over the many years, as in all investigations, it is an ongoing discovery.

Note: As an educator, I always like to take time out for a lessons learned session. On one Halloween tour, we distributed cameras to the crowd. A couple of woman were happy that they thought they'd caught Hank West on film. I said we needed to take it back and analyze it. As much as I hate to have things not be paranormal, I couldn't let it go. The picture they thought they'd captured when looking at the preview screen was not Hank. Rather, it was the pattern of a painting on the wall of the shop that looked amazingly like his profile! Investigators, always analyze data appropriately!

Frank "Hank" West was the night watchman at the old bank and a volunteer fire fighter. Everyone who remembers him says he was a good man.

(Photo courtesy of the Westfield Washington Historical Society.)

ANTI-SLAVERY FRIENDS CEMETERY

West side of North Union Street

For Asa Bales, donating land to Westfield in the 1840s for use as a cemetery couldn't have been more prophetic. He was the first (or second, by some accounts) inhabitant of the new cemetery when a cholera epidemic swept Hamilton County.

The Anti-Slavery Friends Cemetery was tied to a Friends Meeting House of the same name (which burned in a fire in the early 1900s). This group of Quakers believed in upholding the law of God. When the Fugitive Slave Law was enacted, some citizens believed in the law of man, and thought this law should be obeyed. The Anti-Slavery Quakers believed these fugitives were not property and they should be helped.

The cemetery couldn't be more picturesque. It is nestled next to Asa Bales Park, the small rolling hills of the landscape with the cool shade of the black walnut trees that shed their fragrant fruits in fall. As dusk settles or the sun burns off the fog that settles in on certain days during the summer, people swear this quiet spot becomes alive with spirits.

The members of the Anti-Slavery Friends meeting house continued to do so until after the Civil War, eventually with the help of the other Quakers and other members of the community. Today, the meeting house is gone, but the memory of these brave people remains. Or is it just the memory?

We investigated the cemetery and experienced odd things. Strange lights appeared in the first pictures we took. Later, we heard that a Union Civil War soldier was seen along the southwest side of the cemetery.

Our first brush with the dead in this cemetery was when Michael and I were cleaning stones. I was cleaning Samuel S. Pitman's military stone. He was 16 years old in 1862 when he went into Company A, 101st Indiana Infantry, lying about his age. He mustered out on June 24, 1865 as a corporal. He died six months later of lingering dysentery.

The deep shadows dapple the otherwise sunny grove in the Anti-Slavery Friends Cemetery. Stranger shadows dart between the trees at night.

As we looked into the history of the cemetery, which also includes possible abolitionist and slave burials, we also found that a woman in white paces along the southeast section of the cemetery. Some speculation is that she lost her child or its tombstone. She was very active until grave-witching revealed the remnants of a child's tombstone. Now, a woman in white is seen walking into the home which sits on the site of the old Anti-Slavery Friends meeting house. Along the shaded north end, where the shadows of the trees lengthen in the darkness, figures are seen walking among the old stones and occasionally a weeping woman is heard.

Finally, a teenage boy who lives just east of the cemetery usually walked through the cemetery to get to school. One early morning, he was in for the surprise of his life.

Will walked through the cemetery and about a third of the way down he saw a young Union Civil War soldier leaning against a tree. The solider's kit was next to him and he was smoking a cigarette. As Will moved closer, not quite believing what he saw, the soldier turned to him, gave an "up-nod", picked up his gear, flicked the cigarette away and walked toward the south side of the cemetery. Disappearing about half way through. The soldier's description matches Samuel Pitman's description of a young, thin, and soulful person.

Children have reported seeing other children playing ring-around-the-rosy and running in the area only to disappear when approached. Other children have seen a similar soldier walking through the mid part of the cemetery and leaning against a large tree on the east side of the cemetery.

Why all of this unrest? Although the town refuses to acknowledge burials, old-timers told us that the cemetery really extends south of the fence into a wooded area overgrown with scrub trees and poison ivy. In 1970 the Junior Chamber of Commerce was looking for a civic project and decided to clean the stones. After the group was done cleaning them, the stones were stacked. When the Junior Chamber of Commerce members were told they needed to put the stones back where they belonged, they were at a loss. Though there is some debate about the existence of a map, it doesn't seem like anyone knew of it's existence then – or now. The stones remained stacked until 1975. Although I am sure they did their best, many people believe the unrest comes from the fact that these tombstones were moved and not put back in the same spot. But does this explain everything?

When a group of Civil War reenactors decided to try to contact the dead in the cemetery, they got much more than they expected. We had a group of five people. Two women were dressed in period everyday clothes. One man was dressed in period everyday clothes. Another man was dressed as we were, in regular clothes and the last was dressed in a Confederate uniform. First, they were contacted through dowsing rods by a little boy. He told us that a soldier wanted to talk to us. It wasn't, however, the soldier we thought it would be. We were led to James Andrew Jackson's military stone near the tree where the soldier was seen. As the conversation with James Jackson progressed, it became increasingly clear that he was fascinated with the reenactor in the Confederate Uniform. After some coaxing, the man took the dowsing rods and we continued our chat.

We all enjoyed the experience and looked forward to seeing what we could find. We were able to confirm his name and that he returned from the war as a disabled veteran. He was buried in Brownsburg, but his military stone was sent to the cemetery as a memorial for the cause he believed in fighting for.

The next day, the man's wife sent us an e-mail and said he would never go back in that cemetery. He and some of the others said they felt a little ill in the cemetery. When he got home, he found three scratches on his stomach. She said he'd never return.

As a side note, at the Union Street entrance, an Indiana war memorial stands started by CSM Peed, who lived in the house next door until his death. Teenagers report hearing soldiers talking, hearing gun fire and agonized cries. Other visitors to the memorial have smelled gunpowder. One woman reported a white figure walking among the white crosses, bending down every so often as if caring for the area. Some speculate this is CSM Peed. An investigation is ongoing.

The Fallen Hoosier Heroes memorial started by CMS Peed. Before veteran's groups began to help with this effort, the crosses were plain white set directly into the grass.

Luke Frist was the 18th Indiana soldier who died in the line of duty in Iraq. He died January 5, 2004 after suffering burns on 95% of his body in an attack with an improved explosive device in Iraq. One of his fellow unit members said he was "a great soldier and a great man." He was part of the 209th Quartermaster Company, U.S. Army Reserve. Luke was only 20 years old and hoped to work in landscaping after his return home.

PERRY HOME & BALES BARN

West side of North Union Street

From the outside, the house looks just like any other Victorian home, with a few window modifications. With a deck and large yard, this attractive home seems to welcome visitors. The back of the house where a dentist used to have a practice has the beams of Asa Bales' old barn with glass around them. The home was constructed by O.D. Perry in front of the barn and later, an add-on was constructed around the barn.

When I was asked to come in, it was during a home tour. The tour guide, Ana* said I "needed" to come over. As I entered this back area, I noticed not only the hand-hewn beams left over from Asa Bales' barn, but also the extraordinary amount of religious symbols in the room. Everything from menorahs to rich Celtic crosses to Budda and beyond graced one large wall. I thought either something was going on or someone living at the home had a strong interest in collecting religious symbols. I was about to find out.

"Come here." Ana lead me to the basement.

It was a small, well-lit area, used for storage. The plain white rough-plastered walls clearly showed the rough foundation under it. On the north wall was a rough patch job in the shape of a doorway. I looked questioningly at Ana. It was no great secrete that the home was part of the Underground Railroad.

"Do you feel it?" She whispered.

I paused. I could hear the owners and the tour guests upstairs. Then it hit.

The overwhelming the feeling of dizziness. I leaned against the wall. "Oy." I uttered. "I wasn't expecting that."

Ana nodded, "And the cold?"

I certainly didn't feel that but the room was undoubtedly spinning and felt very queasy.

We both agreed it was time to leave and trudged up the stairs. I went to speak with the owners.

Then it got interesting.

The owners were gracious and immediately pointed out the historic relics. "Our religion isn't clear on whether we can come back, or if

The low back side is part of Asa Bales' old barn. When we took this picture, nothing was visible, but we captured a moving anomaly.

what is happening would be something else." Kelly* pointed out, "We thought maybe having a variety of symbols would help."

His wife, Dixie*, was equally open. She showed me around the downstairs, including the cubby under the stairs and the stairs to the second floor. "This is where it started for me," she said.

Her son, Randy*, hadn't wanted to sleep in his room at the head of the stairs. He said it was "too noisy". As a result, Randy slept in their walk-in closet for several years. Dixie told me he didn't like the noises coming from downstairs. During that time, Dixie needed to get into the cupboard. As she withdrew her hand, the door slammed on her pinky, severely bending it permanently.

Over the years they had all noticed items being moved throughout the house. Each believed another person had done the moving. Dixie had an incident in the kitchen. She was making a casserole and mixed all the dry ingredients together. She put them in the oven, just to save time and get them out of the way. She remembered she needed to add one more ingredient and when she reached in the oven, she received second degree burns from the cold oven.

At the end of the tour, the family told us they didn't want an investigation or publicity, something we wholeheartedly understood and abided by. But people started coming to us with stories about the house, and about the surrounding property.

Before the owners bought it, the home had been used as an antique store at one time. The church on the lot next to it used to store overflow items.

It was owned by a couple of men who were frequently gone on buying trips. During one such trip they asked Sarah* to house sit while they were gone. Many times, she saw pieces move through the air. Once, she witnessed an ashtray move from one dresser to another in the living room. But that wasn't to be the most eventful part of the visit.

Almost every evening, Sarah would find the back door unlocked. Usually, she thought she was forgetful. One day, she came down an the door was wide open. Sarah spoke aloud to what she knew was there. She told it that it should stop, because it was a "matter of safety".

The last straw for one of Sarah's guests in the house came one night as they were sitting in the living room. The locked window blew open. They felt a stiff wind blowing. The curtains moved. However, as her friend peered out the window not a branch was moving outside. She promptly packed her bag and left, never to return.

Even before these owners, an earlier owner of the house used to experience footsteps walking down the stairs and lights turning off and on.

The property next door has issues as well. The church which had been used as antique storage and as a theatre, had its spirits too. Sarah saw "things" moving about in the building. Sandi*, another local resident said she saw figures and a glowing light long after anyone would have been in the building.

The former church burned to the ground in 2001. When they cleaned up the debris, they found the other end of the tunnel that ran to the house. It was filled in, history sealed and lost forever. However, that didn't stop the activity. Two young men playing football had their own surprise. Tom threw a pass to Jacob who ran forward to catch it ."It was like I hit a brick wall", he said, shaking his head."I just went down."

Tom agreed, "I went to help him up and we looked for what could have caused it, but found nothing." Upon investigation, we found EMF spikes although there are no electrical lines buried in the area.

Other locals have reported other oddities about this area as well. People have smelled horses, heard the jangle of bits and reins. And a blue light has been seen to hover over the area where the church used to stand.

One possible explanation for the events could be all of the old items had held vibrations of the past and those vibrations created the events. Another could be the ghosts found by other families in the home.

As of this writing, the house stands empty and somewhat forlorn. An occasional light is seen moving about the building late at night. Until another victim, er, *owner* moves in, this house will sit. And wait.

Inside the barn section. The bookshelf contains many different types of religious items. You can see the old hand-hewn barn beams around the bookshelf.

Church on the property next to the house. It was used as an antique store and (albeit briefly) a theater. It burned in 2001. When the rubble was moved, a confirmed tunnel was found to run between the church and the house to the south of it.

(Photo courtesy of the Westfield Washington Historical Society.)

TGI FRIDAYS

14922 US 31

The building was built on Harmon Cox and his wife Katherine's farm ground, as were the shops around it, but for some, Mario's restaurant and the subsequent death of its owner is what they remembered about the building. After Mario's moved out, shortly after the death, the prime real estate stood empty for years.

"Nuts" is what Jackie said the General Manager at TGI Fridays thought she was when she told him about what was going on in the building. Even though the general manager neglects to close by himself. Jeff, who was also a manager frequently heard people walking up and down the stairs.

Trapped is how Jackie felt when she first learned about the spirit activity in the building. She had worked for about six weeks and was the first woman manager to close alone in quite a while. "Things" went on outside the office that chilled her and other workers to the bone.

Once, she was sitting in the office with her shoes off around 2 a.m. and heard banging against the wall. She brushed it off. However shortly after that, she couldn't ignore the fact that someone flicked her on the back of her neck. When she brought it up at the managers' meeting the next day, Chuck, also a manager, said "At least no one is blowing in your ear and playing with your neck."

Managers were not the only members of the staff to experience strange activity. Jenn, one of the bartenders worked late at night. One night, it sounded as though a reggae band was in the kitchen. She walked around the area, not seeing anything amiss but hearing a ladle banging against a pot. She called the general manager who told her to call the police. Instead, she gathered her things and left. The next day, another employee said, "If you think that's something, try hearing all the pots fall over and seeing nothing!"

Marci* was in the bar with the bartender. Both of them heard banging in the walls as though someone was getting a "violent beating". They stayed together that night. When it was time close, they went upstairs to turn off the music together. On the return trip down the stairs, they reached the halfway point and the music started again. They went back up and the sound system was still turned off. Marci yelled, "Shut up!" and the music stopped.

The ghosts of this building seem to have a sense of humor. It is the custom to put the walkie talkies on the base to charge in the evening. Early in the morning, when the store begins to prep items for the day, another employee saw these turn on and heard a woman talking. Lights came on and off all over the building. "Someone was messing with us," she said. Another time, a man's deep voice said, "Boo!" and started laughing.

Other paranormal occurrences include:
- The beer pump started going off without anyone pumping.
- Thanksgiving Day they set up stuff at the bar and left. All the stuff moved by the door.
- Two bartenders heard someone say something laughing and giggling and whistling like it was a joke on them.

For whatever reason, the staff calls the ghost "Katherine". Chuck is sure it is a woman flirting with him. Jackie thinks it is hostile. Jeff has no opinion about the ghost in general, but also feels it is a woman. Girls don't want to be alone. One employee said the manager for Mario's had a heart attack in the building, but this has been proven.

For a time, a manager put up a sign saying "Respect the Ghost" because people were making jokes about it which seemed to make the events happen more often. When recently asked, the manager stated the sign was no longer used and nothing unusual had happened "in months". Corporate story or authentic report? You be the judge.

CHURCH AND POLITICS

130 Penn Street

When Ana* came to me with the story of dirty diapers, I had to laugh. Nowhere in all of my years of ghost hunting had I ever come across a fecal ghost. But, she was serious. "We aren't passing gas," she whispered. "We just smell dirty diapers." Her coworker, Viola*, nodded. "Something is definitely in there."

And why not? The area in which she sat was at one time a church nursery. In fact, the whole building had been several churches at one time. Built in 1854, the Congressional Church occupied the building until it was turned over to the Christ Methodist Church and then to Westfield, which was at the time just a small town.

The building has a great history. During the Civil War, it was used for recruiting soldiers. Because it was centrally located, the church was the point of contact by which all the people of the town came together for news. Even today as the city grows, the building is still used for city council meetings and other civic gatherings.

Many times when Michael and I investigate, we don't just rush in, take pictures and leave. Rather, we gather information, try to piece it together make note of any missing pieces and move forward from that point. As we investigate, we try to make more connections with the hauntings and the past. It is a never-ending delight.

While the town didn't want a full-blown investigation of the building, we nonetheless took every opportunity to gather data when we visited for civic events. During one such meeting, a local woman, whose family runs back many generations confided that she felt that bathroom in the building is "freaky" and that the hall outside of it was "definitely haunted". She, like many others, had gone in to use the one-seater facilities only to hear her name called. Invariably, when those people called went out into the deserted hallway, they were greeted with silence.

Michael and I took the opportunity to see if we could recreate the phenomenon, using each other as a barometer from various parts of the building. Could we actually hear the other from inside the bathrooms? We found that we could not hear anyone inside the offices or inside the large gathering room at the front of the building, but that we could hear people in the hall and the stairway next to it.

When the next opportunity presented itself, we hung out by and in the rest rooms. Sure enough, I heard someone call my name. I exited and asked if either Michael or someone else had called for me. Everyone said no, but that they heard it too.

The building had long been on our tours because of the shadow figures seen in the main room. People from all walks of life had told us they have experienced the shadow people in the room at one time or another. The sightings occurred during all parts of the day. They were described as inky gray figures that would walk between the living, seemingly in another plane and not interacting with anyone.

One man played peek-a-boo with the spirits one morning. He came to work early expecting to get some things done before his hectic day of meetings started. He heard hushed murmurs coming from the front room. He thought that maybe someone was trying to rob the building, so he went to the room, ready to confront the intruders. When he opened the door, the voices stopped. He looked around and found nothing. Shrugging, he closed the door and started to go back to his office. The voices began again. "Just like the humming of cicadas, " he declared, wide-eyed.

Again, he opened the door and again the noises stopped. Closing the door once more, he heard the noise start again. Listening, he heard a variety of people talking. One man, he noted, spoke in old Quaker plain-speak. "It was then I realized these must be spirits of the people who helped found this city." He shrugged, "And why not? They had a lot of work to do." He opened the door one last time and said, "You go about your business. I've got my work to do too." He closed the door and walked back to his office. When he heard the noises in the future, "I felt calmed because I knew who it was and knew that they were just working, the same as I was."

Our tours have had their share of experiences as well. One Halloween night, a particularly high-spirited group attended the tour. Dressed as ghosts, they had already scared some trick-or-treaters by coming out of the cemetery dressed as ghosts. However, it was one skeptical man in particular who was terrified by what he saw.

I'd told the stories and the group started looking inside the building through the windows. I was walking with the skeptic, but looking in the windows myself when I saw something. I asked him to shine his flashlight in and he said, "You saw it too." I asked him to tell me what

The old Congressional Church, later used as the Westfield Town Hall. The building to the left is the minister's home.

(Photo courtesy of the Westfield Washington Historical Society)

The City Hall as it looks today. Visitors see various spirits and shadows. They also hear voices from unseen entities.

he'd seen, because I wasn't at all sure I was completely comfortable with what I thought I saw.

He described the entity: "I saw a man looking north with a bowl hair cut. I could see wisps of hair on his forehead, the bridge of his nose and the curve of his upper lip." He indicated the man's head was directly under a clock in the building.

I asked everyone to stop and then we tried to recreate the shadow man, as no one saw him but us. We couldn't recreate him through light and the reflection of any person's head. Mr. Skeptic, who was subdued the rest of the tour, shook my hand at the end and said, "I will never look at the paranormal the same way ever again."

But that wasn't to be all. On a subsequent Halloween night, a self-proclaimed sensitive shouted out, "Ok, it just needs to stop!" during our visit to this location. At first I thought he meant me. Then he said, "I can feel them." About that time, the blinds flipped up in two rooms on separate floors. In unison.

If that wasn't enough, only a handful of us saw it happen. Others said the blinds had not moved or were still down. The sensitive said there was an African-American man looking out at us. Only he saw this man.

We were called in one day to deal with an emergency. Ana had been working alone and swore she'd seen a ghost. "I hate to sound cheesy, but it was like it was a shirt on a clothesline, held up by the arms with clothespins." After asking her the usual questions to rule out any man-made cause, we agreed to meet and see if we couldn't do a little communication with the spirit.

Later that same week, I brought my recording device and started asking questions, explaining that its current communication was causing distress. We played the recording back. I heard something and so did my companion, who asked to hear it again. When we played it back, we distinctly heard "It's me!" in kind of a mocking way, as if to say "Duh, didn't you get it the first time?"

"That's Camilia!" She exclaimed.

Camilla Axelrod was a community mainstay. She worked for the town, owned and operated a beauty salon and owned one of the most beautiful Underground Railroad houses in town. People either loved her because of her kind and generous spirit or hated her because they thought she was a busy-body. However, most agreed that regardless of their personal feelings toward her, she would give anyone, even an

Camilla Allen Axelrod: One of the many voices of the building.

(Photo courtesy of the Westfield Washington Historical Society.)

enemy the shirt off her back if he or she needed it badly enough.

Ana distinctly felt that the Axelrod collection at the historical society was the reason for the visit. It was moldering away without a home. And this visit from Camilla was the catalyst to jumpstart the historical society's museum efforts.

As we stood talking, we clearly smelled diesel fuel. We traced the smell into a copier room where it disappeared. Both of us were stymied because Camilla didn't deal in diesel. I filed this information away. Many weeks and months passed. We began to receive reports of a tall, bald, fairly young man who was seen going down the west stairs and into the basement of the building. My first reaction was asking Ana who had recently died that was tied to the town. Her answer was a firefighter. Chad Hittle was killed in an off-duty truck crash in his personal vehicle. I asked if we had a picture of the man and sure enough, he shaved his head, was well built and fit the descriptions we'd received of the phantom grey man.

Currently this building is still a hotbed of activity. The firefighter is still seen and the conversations still happen in the large front meeting room. Additionally, activity seems to have reached outside the building.

One 13-year old young man was walking on the west side of the building. He went up the handicapped ramp and down the stairs. As he descended, his arm was pulled back by an unknown source. Another teenager while imitating this act, was summarily pushed down the stairs.

Mike*, a firm and happy believer in the paranormal, was on our tour recently. As we talked about all the wonderful events in the building, he walked to the east side handicapped ramp and looked in the window. Although he didn't see anything, he felt very ill. As we moved on to our next stop, he said his arm really hurt. I asked if he'd been touched or something. He said he didn't think so. Finally he pulled his shirt sleeve up because the pain was so bad. On his forearm were three fresh, bloody scratches.

I'll file this one away too and fit the pieces together when it's time.

The stairway where a teenager was touched by unseen hands.

THE JOKE'S ON YOU!

301 East Main Street (State Road 32)

The building is neatly kept and currently for sale. Most people wouldn't even suspect that under the grey and white exterior of the small building a host of history took place.

The White family came to Westfield to settle the land much as the city's founders to support the Indiana branch of the Underground railroad. In the 1850s, when the Underground Railroad was reaching a fever pitch, this building at the southeast corner of Cherry Street was a small inn. Humble and comfortable overnight accommodation and home cooked meals were a large draw to this small establishment. Little did most of the guests realize that below them and sometimes with them, lurked fugitives from the South.

The Compromise of 1850 included several bills to appease the north and south and to stave off a civil war. One of these bills, the Fugitive Slave Act, demanded that citizens aid in the capture of escaped slaves, which made it almost impossible for free slaves in the north to maintain their lives. Over 20,000 free blacks moved to Canada after the Compromise of 1850 was enacted. The fugitives heading north through the Underground Railroad followed suit.

Westfield was a small part of that effort. Slave hunters knew that if they didn't capture the fugitives before they got to Westfield, it would be almost useless to try getting them back because the people of the town believed the fugitives should be free. However around this time, there was dissent amongst the people. Part of the community split into those who believed in the law of man and upheld the Fugitive Slave Act. The others believed in the law of God and thought these fugitives should be helped, not hindered.

During this time Lavica White received two fugitives, a woman and her daughter. They knew the hunters were behind them. They could hear the dogs. Mrs. White hid the two ladies and sent word to her son, Michajah White. No sooner had she done that then sure enough, the slave hunters came to her door asking if she'd seen the pair.

Mrs. White had to think quickly. The only way out of the building at the time was the door they came in. Mrs. White commiserated with the men and said, "You must be dreadfully hungry. You sit here and let me fix you something."

As the men sat down to wait, Mrs. White dressed the fugitives in her and her daughters clothing. As they were Quakers, their dresses came high up on their necks and down to their wrists. The ladies also donned gloves and Quaker bonnets with large panels around their face to shield them from the sun.

Mrs. White placed steaming heaps of meat and potatoes in front of the men. Her son came to the door and said he was ready to pick up their visitors. Astoundingly, in front of the men, the two women were led through the room and out the front door. Michajah whisked the ladies away. Although it can't be confirmed, it is reported that the ladies made their way to Canada, where they lived long, happy lives.

This story is supported by the original floor plan of the simple building. Additionally, the floor joists are made of half round poplars and there are large wooden half round poplar benches in the basement.

Originally, the owners didn't feel as though they had any stories, but after some remodeling, which is said to bring out spirits by the disruption in familiarity, they changed their mind.

They would work late into the night and several times, while in the basement, they would see black shadows pacing back and forth in the basement. While neither felt intimidated, they did feel as though someone was waiting for something. A ride to another stop on the underground railroad, perhaps?

But shadows weren't the only indication of spirits. Often times, the owners would hear footsteps in the shop at night, long after they were closed. Every time they would investigate they would find nothing. Finally, they installed a bell. The spirit is evidently playful as they would hear the bell and still find no one upstairs. One evening, they heard the bell, went upstairs and found nothing. They checked the door and found it locked. They went downstairs and immediately heard the door slam. Running upstairs, they found no one and the door was still locked. They returned to the basement and heard someone stomping upstairs in a random pattern. They ran once more upstairs just in time to see the door swing open and close. They went to it again and the door was unlocked, yet they found no one outside.

This couple isn't the only owner to experience paranormal activity. When the building was used for lawn mower repair and blade sharpening, the owner at that time had his own experience.

He was very good at his job and could fix anything. He had never had anything come to him that was unable to be fixed, yet for six weeks, a lawn mower repair eluded him. Finally, he gave up. As the owner of the mower came to pick it up, the store owner said, "Let me give it one more try." When he went into the back, he tried once more to fix the mower by doing the same thing he'd been doing. It worked and the mower was fixed. Paranormal or not, the store owner was mystified.

Today, the building stands alone and for sale. I often wonder if the ghosts are still active and waiting for the next occupants.

Formerly The Cottage, this building still has the residual activity of fugitives from the South.

TALBERT HOUSE

East side of North Union in front of Christ Methodist Church

The O.E.Talbert Lumber Company was located in Westfield. Harry Talbert took over the business from O.E. and the rest of the family. At one time his wealth was enough that he "owned most of downtown Westfield in one form or another" according to his great-granddaughter. This business afforded Harry the opportunity to build a beautiful brick home in the late 1930s. It was built of the finest materials. Brick walls, ample windows, beautiful hard wood floors and arched doorways graced the house. A small bay sunny nook jutted out on the south side. Originally this home boasted a wrought iron fence with brick pillars around it. Several types of trees shaded the property. Harry, his wife Ruth and his family enjoyed a good life in Westfield. He expanded his business into several towns including Noblesville, Sheridan, Carmel, Rensselaer and Warsaw.

Some people believe it is Harry haunting the home. Harry loved the home and lived in it until he moved to the Colonial Crest Convalescent Center in Indianapolis where he died at aged 91 in 1980.

Other people believe it may be his father's business partner and brother-in-law, Orlando D. Haskett. Mr. Haskett was raised in Westfield in the Quaker faith by his father Daniel who had an on-again/off-again relationship with the meeting house. During the Civil War, Daniel had believed in following the law of God and helping fugitives from the South. He broke from his Quaker roots and joined the effort. He also became a member of the Masonic Lodge, which did not sit well with the Quakers.

This type of free thinking led Orlando to go west to work on a cattle and corn farm but he eventually returned to his roots and farming. He settled back in Indiana and married Elma Talbert and had a daughter, Reba. Once part of the Talbert family, Orlando became a lumber magnet all over the US and eventually started his own lumber business in Indianapolis in 1920, O.D. Haskett Lumber. Like his father, he was a member of the Masonic lodge as well as several others, including the Ancient Landmarks Lodge, Ancient Free and Accepted Masons, Reaper Commandry, Knights Templars, Murat Temple of the Mystic Shrine, Modern Woodsmen of America, and Knights of Pythias (Cicero, Indiana). Orlando wanted very much to be a self-made man, but he also worked closely with the O.E. Talbert Lumber Company whenever possible.

Ghosts have long since been rumored at this home. If its imposing façade and gorgeous shade trees weren't enough, the tall spiky rails of the iron fence that surrounded it would have been enough to spark stories. For many years, it's been owned by the Christ Methodist Church. When it became home to Student Impact for a few years, the children that attended the day camp always said that different parts of the house put them ill at ease.

The basement, which wasn't used except for storage, was something that all the children wanted to avoid. When asked to go into it, most of them would find a reason not to go. My daughter, Brittany, went downstairs and declared it "creepy" as did my objective son and many of the other children. A camp counselor told me she saw a woman fitting the description of Harry's wife in the upper floor.

"I was walking up the stairs. As I got to the top, I turned to the left. A transparent woman breezed out of one of the rooms, walked past me and turned down the stairs. When I looked on the stairs, she was gone."

For years there has been talk of destroying this building to make more parking and make the church more accessible. Perhaps what roams the halls of the house might move into the church if this does happen.

Early photo of the Talbert family's lumber company.

(Photo courtesy of the Westfield Washington Historical Society)

The Talbert House today. It is owned by the Christ Methodist Church and hosts several types of activities. Hopefully the spirits approve!

WE HAVE A SERIAL KILLER?

At first, there was not much outcry against the number of gay men that disappeared from the Indianapolis area. When more and more gay men were reported missing and the gay community began to whisper about foul play and the police stood at attention.

Herbert Baumeister was a successful businessman. His Sav-a-Lot Thrift stores served the needy of the area. Beneath his nonchalant exterior lurked the heart of an alleged killer. During his teen years, his behavior became anti-social. He was eventually diagnosed with schizophrenia but no prescribed treatment seemed to be carried out. Back when he was diagnosed, sometimes these things were just swept under the carpet. He went to college but never graduated and went through a series of jobs that supposedly his father helped him into.

Finally he married Julianna Saiter in 1971 and had three children: Marie, Erich and Emily. Julie left her job as a teacher to have the children and supplemented the family's income with odd jobs. Herbert started work at a thrift store, after having been fired for urinating on a letter at the BMV office. Three years later, they opened the first Sav-a-Lot store. Within three years, the couple was able to buy an 18 acre farm, named Fox Hollow Farms in Westfield, Indiana. With an indoor swimming pool, a stable and beautiful rolling hills, it was perfection.

Until the couple started having marital problems.

Herbert was domineering and Julie (albeit reluctantly) deferred to him in decision making. This is probably part of the reason in 1994 when their son Erich found a skeleton in the backyard, she bought the story of it being one of Herbert's fathers old medical skeletons. As the marriage deteriorated, the family spent less time with Herbert. This left him free to play games.

One such time, Tony Harris, a friend of Roger Goodlet who was one of the men who was missing, ended up with Herbert at his home. Herbert said his name was Brian Smart. When they arrived at the house, Tony was horrified by the mannequins posed around the indoor pool. Herbert told Tony that they kept him company because he was "lonely". After a harrowing experience with auto-erotic asphyxiation, in which Herbert almost choked Tony to death, Tony convinced Herbert to take him home. After this event, Tony went to the police who staked out the 501 Tavern in the Indianapolis neighborhood of Chatham Arch where Herbert said he wanted to meet Tony the next week. But Herbert didn't show up.

When Indianapolis police brought suspicions to the Hamilton County law enforcement, according to some sources, Hamilton County wasn't interested in pursuing the issue. Authorities couldn't believe that anyone in the area would do something so heinous. Meanwhile, Julie and Herbert's marriage was ending. Their business was failing and by June 1996 they were well on their way to divorce. With the divorce in the works, Julie called the police about the bones her son had found. Herbert was out of town with her son and it was the perfect time.

At first Hamilton County law enforcement believed the whole notion wasn't true. According to some sources, Captain Tom Anderson of the County Sheriff's office said the whole idea was "bullshit". Nevertheless, Julie led them through the yard and the men began to kick up dirt. Imagine their surprise when they began kicking up bone fragments and teeth. Still not convinced, they bagged up some evidence and sent it to Indiana University where the fragments and teeth were confirmed to be recently extracted, burned human remains.

More digging and more evidence was collected. Law enforcement contacted Herb at Lake Wawasee. Herbert gave up his son without a struggle, thinking it was a divorce game and not because of his evening activities. Initially over 5,000 human remains were collected, most belonging to only four bodies. In a ditch between the Baumeister property and their neighbor's, spines, ribs and other assorted bones were found. Another seven men were identified from these remains. Later analysis showed that some victims were burned right away and others were allowed to decompose before they were burned.

Shortly after Herbert gave up his son, he figured out the jig was up and took off for Port Huron with the help of a loan from his older brother, Brad. Brad was unaware of the whole cemetery-in-my-yard situation until after he'd given his brother money. Herbert moved through Sarnia and on to Grand Bend, Ontario. On July 2, 1996 he was awakened by a Canadian law official and asked what he was doing sleeping under a bridge. He said he was just grabbing some rest before he moved on. The policewoman noticed the baggage and video tapes in his back seat. The next day in Pinery Park, Herbert shot himself in the head with a .357 Magnum revolver. Herbert stated in a note that he was offing himself because of his failed business and marriage. He did not acknowledge the dead people in his yard, nor were the videos ever found.

But, there is more. It's been suggested that Herbert Baumeister was the I-70 killer during the early 1990s. The killings stopped shortly before the men began disappearing in Indianapolis. And according to records, he was in the areas when the murders happened. But as of now, no final determination has been made. Additionally, bones were found in 1995 in the woods across from 4533 Old Vincennes Road, off Interstate 64 near U.S. 150 in Floyds Knob in Floyd County. It was suspected the bones belonged to an Indianapolis man, Jerry Williams-Comber, who went missing around the same time. Law enforcement suspect Herbert Baumeister murdered him as well.

Admittedly, I have not been on the grounds of this property. Since the murders, the house has changed hands at least three times. Today it is home to a family who has made it very clear with "NO TRES-PASSING" signs that intruders are not welcome. Michael and I don't go where we don't have permission or are not invited. However, several people and paranormal groups have set bad examples and have tres-passed on the property. Something I hope stops.

People who have had permission have related stories to me. Law enforcement doesn't like to talk about things they can't see. "If it's not there, it's not real." Is a common phrase I hear. My own son, Chris-topher, who is in training to be an MP doesn't believe in what isn't real.

Nevertheless, several law enforcement personnel report strange goings on in the pool area. Regular checks of the area when it stood empty were done. A law enforcement officer said that it was "creepy to walk by". When Deana* shone her light into the pool area, which still had water in it, she said it wasn't hard to imagine what went on.

Another policeman said he patrolled the house once and he saw white figures walking in the pool area. "At first, I thought my light was causing it, but it wasn't. I doused it and the figures were still walking. Suddenly one came from behind, running, and they both fell. I watched them fall and disappear."

The main area in which the bodies were dumped is one of the prettiest and wildest places. At one time long before the murders, trains would have chugged by this area. Today, people walk their dogs, run and listen to music, and roller blade down the trail that borders the property. The Monon Trail creates a picturesque setting to something that is so tragic and senseless.

These are not the only spirits that remain. One of the victim's relatives, Robert* contacted me over a year ago. We had a really good conversation. Basically the relative stated that the victim was seen as an apparition in the relative's house the night he was murdered. The relative wanted to know if it would do any good to go out to the location where the bones were found. He also wanted to know if the victim may be attached to the area because of what happened and what were the chances that the relative could see the victim. Obviously I couldn't give an exact answer. I encouraged the relative to seek out the answers the questions for closure's sake as answers from Herbert Baumeister were taken with him in death.

It is my hope that all the victims of this outrageous and heinous atrocity rest peacefully.

House where the murders took place.

This valley is one of the areas where the killer discarded the victims.

OUR WELCOME

We moved into the small unassuming Westfield house as a result of our move back from Germany. We had been rehabbing a house in Terre Haute for a friend who was going to use it as a rental. Since we helped rehab, we paid no rent, which was a good thing, as gas, even at its low prices back in 2000 was eating our meager budget.

Finally, the commute to Indianapolis coupled with the lack of jobs in the Queen City lead us to the home on Northbrook Circle. It had great energy and good flow in the front of the house. A keeping room and office, and kitchen were airy and comfortable.

The back of the house was a different story. A pokey hall that ran the length of the house ended in the master bedroom with a private bath. It was a room that spanned the width of the house. It was a cool quiet room with gorgeous shade trees out both windows. We loved lazy days of waking up to the wind rustling the trees and the plethora of birds that lived in the seven different types of trees on the property.

Despite our interest in the paranormal, we were truly surprised to find this house haunted. Our time in it was very pleasant. The home was built in the 1960s and had been updated in the 1980s and 1990s. Still, it retained some of the dark wood and paneling features from its early days.

As we settled in, we found items going missing only to be found in other rooms. Early on, we thought we just hadn't unpacked the items and thought nothing of it. Once, we were looking for a Phillips head in a set of screwdrivers and we couldn't find it, no matter how hard we looked. Eventually, we found it in the back of the top most cabinet in the kitchen, one we had yet to fill with our possessions.

The true meaning of the word "haunted" came when we heard noises coming from our bedroom. At first, we thought it was simply the washer, the fireplace, shifting boxes or something else. However one evening we were enjoying a fire in the keeping room. It was gloriously warm and we were listening to music. Both of us heard a huge bang, loud enough to rattled the windows.

Peering outside, we saw nothing. We looked at each other. I looked down the hall. A woman was slowly floating from west to east in our bedroom. She had a long brown shirt and a cream-colored long sleeved blouse. Her brown-blonde hair was piled up in a bun and she seemed to be carrying something in her hands like a bucket.

I took off down the hall, leaving a questioning Michael in my wake. When I entered the room, I found it freezing. We were used to the fire heating almost all the way to our room and we liked the room cool. However, I could see my breath– and no sign of the lady, or anything out of place that would have contributed to the noise.

Afterward, as we researched the property, we found a farm house stood on the property. Perhaps she was coming into the house or barn.

We moved out due to many issues related to maintenance of the house. For months it remained empty only inhabited for short periods of time over the next few years. Every now and then, we go by the home and wonder if the woman is still banging around the home. Recently, someone more permanent moved. We hope life is as interesting for the new inhabitants as it was for us.

Note: Many cities are called "The Queen City". Terre Haute and Cincinnati to name just two.

Looking somewhat forlorn, one can only wonder if the woman still paces the back room.

ONE HUNDRED YEAR WAIT

21617 Hinkle Road

Hinkle's Creek in Washington Township was settled in the early 1830s by several families of friends having come from Pennsylvania, North Carolina and Tennessee. As early as 1833, meetings were held for worship in the various homes. These meetings were continued until an organization was effected in June 1836 at which time a log home was built for the Friends "Preparative Meeting", which was a branch of the Westfield Monthly meeting. In the 1840s, it became a Monthly Meeting. On the "First Day" and "Fifth Day" of each week, no matter the distance or the condition of the weather, people faithfully attended, or risked an "intervention". The first trustees were James Harris, Jacob Carson and Samuel Sumner. They purchased 3.4 acres from Joseph Sumner for the permanent location at a whopping cost of $13.50.

The first Hinkle Creek meeting house (the "'s" was dropped in the 1930s) was destroyed by fire in the 1852. This building stood until 1872 when it burned and replaced the same year by the current building. This new building originally contained two rooms, one for the men and one for the women to conduct business during the meeting. During the worship part of the meeting, the men sat on one side of the bigger room and the women on the other.

At the north side of the room, four "gallery" seats faced the audience. They were used for ministers and officials. Someone was always in charge of the meeting to open and close the service. This simple building was largely taken care of by donated materials and labor from members of the Monthly Meeting. Over the years, old windows have been replaced and a basement installed for dining and social purposes.

The dress of the members was very plain. Gray and brown were for dress up and black was for mourning or funerals in plain clothes. Men wore dark hats and the women wore the gray, brown or black bonnets. Any violation of the rules of the church or dress code was grounds for counseling, reprehension or disownment by the church,

The main part of the meeting for worship was silent meditation which sometimes lasted for an hour or two with prayer and personal witness. The meeting would end when the head of the meeting and stood and shook hands with those next to him. The other members

The former Hinkle Creek Friends Meeting House. Area residents say that there are more than just tombstones in the cemetery.

followed the procedure and the church service was over. Today, meditation periods are much shorter, but the original meeting idea remains
largely the same.

The cemetery by the meeting house was originally kept by the
members and the trustees of Hinkle Creek meeting house. The meeting has an interest bearing fund for the maintenance of the cemetery,
insuring its permanent care. The first funeral was the young daughter
of James and Nancy Fisher in 1836. One of the members, Henry Bray,
helped dig the grave. The first burials were in the southeast section of
the cemetery although this information cannot be verified as this section of the cemetery was never plotted. During the early formation of
this church, the dead were hauled on wagons through the trails to the
church. It seems that the families simply chose a spot and the hired
grave diggers dug east to west, north to south or haphazardly in a
direction. Small slab stones with the names and dates cut into them
faced all directions. The ground was never leveled. Some people made
their own coffins. The favored wood was white or black walnut or white
oak because they lasted the longest. Later wooden boxes were set in
the grave and the coffins lowered into them. By the 1920s concrete and
metal vaults were in use.

Around this same time, the trustees held a meeting in which
they decided to level and start a system that would make the cemetery
easier to maintain. The small markers were pulled, the ground leveled
and seeded, and the grave markers were reset in rows. The markers show the burials, but not where the owner of the stone is buried.
In 1930, Thomas E. and Laura Ramsey donated adjacent land to the
north for more burials. According to the 1958 records, 499 burials had
been recorded.

In the early days, the modes of transportation were walking,
riding horse back, wagon or buggy. The trails were quite rough. The
people of the community were neighborly and worked together in planting, harvesting, clearing land, and in building homes. When sickness
and death came, the people shared with those in need for the benefit
of all. In 1986 a dead pine tree with 167 rings was removed from the
property, showing that it was there to witness it all. People who settled
in this section had good soil for farming, virgin black and white walnut, sugar maple, yellow poplar and oak trees. Hunting was also plentiful with bear, deer, wolves, cougar, coon, small game and wild turkey.
Legend even has it that Henry Bray killed the last bear in the Hamilton

County area.

In fact, Reverend Amos Carson recollected when he was 86 that when Jacob Carson, his grandfather died that the amount of the funeral totaled $7.50 to which he commented, 'It was cheaper to die then, than it is now."

The meeting house has always been rooted in consideration of others. Phoebe Lindley Doan of Westfield recollected in 1926 that she spent her time in this church for Sunday School, often walking three miles or more to reach the church. Additionally, before Indiana set up an education infrastructure, Hinkle Creek conducted classes for both girls and boys and studied grammar, arithmetic, reading, spelling, history and writing. Later, The Opportunity School of the Mentally Retarded and Handicapped was organized by some members of Hinkle Creek Meeting. It was one of he first model schools in the State of Indiana and has for many years, been incorporated into the public school systems we see today.

Records were lost prior to 1850 in a safe-blowing at the Westfield meeting house. Although the motive was supposedly money and no one was arrested, it was blamed on the Indians that lived in the woods around Cool Creek. Meeting house records show that not only were the members concerned for "people of color" but they also had a committee for "Indian concerns" which helped feed, clothe and educate Native Americans in the area. Eventually Methodists started attending the meetings and later became the Hinkle Methodist Church due to Methodists having only one more vote than the Society of Friends.

The area is one of the most beautiful in Hamilton County. Quiet and serene, neighbors around the church have unanimously stated that they all used to play "Ding Dong Ditch", tag and freeze tag in the neighborhood and cemetery at night for well over 50 years. "It was the thing to do and as kids we loved it. Our kids still love it." One man smiled. "We saw a lot of stuff in there [the cemetery]."

Some of the many reports from neighbors include misty figures and figures darting from stone to stone. "I realize when we played tag in the dark, that what we saw could have been one of the players and nothing paranormal," Emily shrugged, "but when you're playing in broad daylight and you see black shapes moving from stone to stone, you kind of take notice."

In our investigations of the cemetery, we captured a mist taking shape in early evening. Michael and I had a feeling as if something

A glimpse at a place that is peaceful, but full of spirit activity.

A close up (lower left) of a mist forming in the back of the picture near the tree. This photo was captured on our Hamilton County bus tour.

was watching us. It was so strong we felt like something was ready to touch or rush us. When we snapped the picture, it was clear even on the small camera viewer that something was forming. Although we did not get EVPs during the session or make any further contact, the idea that something is in the cemetery is compelling.

Additionally, during one of our tours, we had a pre-teen boy attend. He was very much into the paranormal. He spoke very matter of factly about seeing spirits around him. Throughout the tour, he said that there was a spirit on the bus that someone else brought with her. He was also very careful to ask the spirits not to come with us when we left locations. When we arrived at the cemetery, he said the children in the cemetery missed their parents. I asked him why they were still in the cemetery if they had already crossed. He told me, "They know they are dead, but for some reason, they can't connect with their parents for a certain amount of time." I asked him how long ago some of the children had died and he said, "One hundred years." Then he nodded to the north edge of the cemetery and said, "There's a child over there with his father. He just came to get him." Although none of us on the tour could see the same thing the boy did, we did find it an interesting perspective from one child to another. And how clearly this boy communicated what he saw and what he was told by the spirits.

Finally, as a footnote, the hauntings are not confined to the cemetery. One of the split level homes across the street has its own ghost. An older gentleman is heard stomping in the second level when family members are in the lower level. Only one child has seen him walking from room to room. One woman got so used to the sounds that when her husband came home one night and wanted to know what the noises were, she just said, "It's the old man." When pressed the woman told her husband of all the times she'd been alone and heard the noises. Her husband never brought it up again. But that's a different story for a different day.

This wooded area on the north side of the cemetery is where a young boy said many children wait before they are reunited with their parents in the afterlife.

LITTLE NEAL KNIGHT

South Union Street, across from Valley Farms Drive

Summit Lawn Cemetery is very quiet. Nestled in the suburb of Westfield, surrounded on two sides by woods, this unassuming cemetery seems to be developing a haunted history of its own.

When Michael and I moved to Hamilton County, we had a ball the first couple of years just driving the roads and discovering all of the cemeteries we could. With the online GIS system through the county, we didn't have to look so hard after a couple of years. Still, we learned quickly how creepy even the simplest of cemeteries could be.

Michael and I routinely visit and help preserve cemeteries. We find them to be a great place to walk, to think, to talk to each other and a great place for history. We knew Summit Lawn was fairly new in our scheme of cemetery visits, but its beauty far surpassed that tiny detail. When we first visited it, I was creating an artsy movie for my undergraduate degree. I took a lot of video footage and made a movie about life and death. During the filming, I focused on a gorgeous old angel statue marking one of the oldest graves. Unfortunately, a couple of years later, the cemeteries in Westfield experienced vandalism and the beautiful angel was beheaded. The head was never found.

I try to locate graves for people looking for their ancestors. On one occasion as I attempted to find a grave, I was greeted by a girl with long black hair and a dark uniform. I said hello to her but she said nothing to me. I started to make a wide circle around her just to keep some distance and suddenly, she had moved 100 yards away from me, crouched in the woods. She gave off a vibe that was so strong, it told me I was not welcome, just as much as the snide look on her pale face. That particular day, I decided to take my leave.

I am not the only person to have odd experiences in the woods. Raejean*, whose grandmother is buried in the woods said that she often goes by the cemetery at night and sees lights "flash over the cemetery all the time".

Another odd experience was shortly after the vandalism had taken place. I went in because I'd heard of a woman who had lost the angel from a relative's grave. I thought I had a picture left over from my film that I would give her but I wanted to see if the 110 year old angel on little Neal Knight's grave had been damaged. I wandered around the cemetery unable to find it again and spoke with a lawn care professionals who were cutting the grass. They told me "none of these graves have ever had angels on them." Odd talk considering I had video of at least one angel and another woman had a picture of the angel sitting on her mother's grave. Later I went back and found poor Neal Knight's Italian marble life size angel headless with broken wings.

Even the people who live in the apartments nearby have issues. One tenant, George*, said that he saw a small child playing around the cemetery at night. He was a "glowing milk white". In his culture, he is taught to "leave the dead to the dead."

His friend, Anthony said, "Many times, we'll be talking outside with friends in the evening and we see white figures walking among the stones." He's convinced there is more than tombstones in the cemetery at any given time.

And why not? Some of Westfield's elite are buried in the cemetery, among them Camilla Axelrod and Hank West (see the bank story in this book). Natalie Wheeler, for whom the Natalie Wheeler Trail is named, is also buried in this cemetery. Natalie Wheeler was a young girl, happy-go-lucky and free spirited who died suddenly at age ten due to complications of a respiratory illness.

Some paranormal investigators believe this cemetery is haunted because of the graves moved from the Old Friends Cemetery (see the story in this book) to Summit Lawn. The bodies were moved, but the location of them at Summit Lawn is not known, nor are the grave markers present. What happened to the grave markers and where are the bodies?

Are any of these people responsible for the hauntings? We don't know. However even on a sunny day, the cloying sense of darkness creeps over this sunny site making it somewhat less peaceful than it appears.

Little Neal Knight's beautifully carved Italian Marble stone. Abused by the elements and vandals, little Neal may be one of the spirits that roam the cemetery.

I SAW THE DEVIL, OK?

South Union Street, north of Midland Trail

Some people believe places with high emotion or disturbances are haunted or more haunted than most. Nothing would be more true than the Old Friends Cemetery. Originally, the cemetery belonged to the Westfield Friends meeting House.

This area has had much unrest. Behind the main part of the cemetery is a wooded area which many people believe are home to graves as well. In the 1950s and 60s a scientist and his family had a home in this area, without heat or electricity. Some people believed there was more than academic science happening in the shack and more "crazy wizardry". The Women's Club turned the cemetery into the Martha Doan Memorial Garden in honor of the Westfield woman with the same name (also buried in Summit Lawn Cemetery).

Martha Doan was an "interesting, vivacious, out-going lady" who was "blessed with good health" and "vigorous and active" with a keen mind and alert presence until she died. She was one of seven children born to her parents, Abel and Phoebe (Lindley) Doan. Her original house was at the southeast corner of US 31 and State Road 32. It is now at Conner Prairie as part of an exhibit. Martha attended the Westfield Friends meeting house and the Friends Union High Academy. Her parents (and Quakers in general) were progressive. Education for women was an important part of their lives. Martha received a Bachelors and Masters from Purdue and a literature degree from Earlham. In 1896 she was the first woman to receive a doctoral degree from Cornell University. Martha taught high school and college for her entire life, starting at Manual Training High School, then Vasssar College and rising to Dean of Women at Earlham and Iowa Wesleyan. In her later years, she moved back to her family's home and helped the community through friendship, donations, and gift-giving.

In making this cemetery into a park-like setting, a gazebo and benches were placed in the cemetery after the tombstones were semi-removed. For certain this place has unrest. During a second renovation recently, it was found during the revamping of some drainage that when the original drainage was put in, some poor burial was disturbed. The bones were just shoved out of the way and the drain put in. During the second renovation these bones were handed over to an archaeologist for timeline analysis.

The stories from this area resonate from the Underground Railroad times. On the north east side of the cemetery back in the woods, children used to play in a dugout that belonged to the basement of the Howe Homestead. This home was used as part of the Underground Railroad. Stories handed down to generations state that when slave hunters visited the house, the fugitives were taken from the basement, out of the cave and through the creek to the Lindley home in the northwest part of Washington Township.

Children who used to play in this dugout said that it was completely dark. At one time someone had installed an overhead light, but the wires had been cut and at any time of the day, the darkness became all-enveloping. Games of blind tag, secret club initiations, and séances were some of the activities the kids remember.

At once such séance, Roger* remembers trying to contact former fugitives.

"We didn't know what we were doing. It was something we'd do, going in that cave. We just thought that it would be fun to try and conjure something up. That evening, there were four of us- me and a three friends- Alan, Paul* and Fred*. We were seniors in high school, looking forward to the summer. We started with the usual- we wanted them to come out, make their presence know. We were trying to scare each other, egging each other on.*

Suddenly, a breeze came through. At first, we didn't think anything about it. But it became a torrent of wind, you know, like a wind storm. The pointer started going nuts. Now, you can say it was the wind, but it was moving counter to the wind. It started spelling out things. It spelled "'Jacob' and 'die' and then it spelled 'soon'.

That freaked us all out and we tried to get out. Whatever was in there, wouldn't let us out. We struggled so hard to get out, we finally made it to the wall and inched our way out. When we got out, we saw it was still swirling inside. But it was still as the grave outside. All of us took off back to my house.

Howe Homestead (razed). This building was rumored to have a tunnel from the home to Cool Creek.

(Photo courtesy of the Westfield Washington Historical Society)

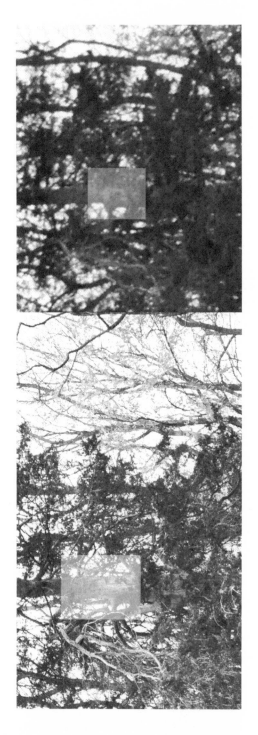

The face in the picture on the right was captured at night. The picture on the left twas captured the next day at the same location.

We must have tried to figure it out most of the evening. Finally, Alan said he didn't want to talk about it anymore. We pressed him a little and he said, 'I saw the face of the devil tonight, ok?' and he clammed up. To this day, Alan won't talk about it.

The next morning, Paul, Fred and I went back out. Alan refused to go. Our Ouija board was absolutely destroyed. And the plastic pointer was imbedded in the wall, right behind where Alan would have been sitting.

The worst thing was that what the board said came true. Jacob, Alan's brother, did die. Alan knew he was being drafted but hadn't told anyone. He was sent to Vietnam and was killed on his first mission out."

This experience wasn't the only incident near the cemetery. Once the cemetery was made into a memorial park, people reported seeing ghostly white shadows sitting on a bench under the young pine tree. During one of our investigations, we did not see any figures, but we did capture the picture of a face in one of the trees. We went back out the next day to see if it was just a bark pattern, and could find nothing to indicate this.

Some paranormal investigators and others who have seen this photo believe that it is the spirit of one of the people buried in the cemetery. Others believe it is a spirit guide who watches over the area. Still others believe that there is more than one protector in the trees of the cemetery.

COOL CREEK

2000 East 151st Street

Cool Creek Park is one of the nicest parks in Hamilton County. The 90 acres of woods and 4 miles of trails is perfect for anyone who loves the outdoors. This park is heavily used at all times of the year, due in part to the ideal roads for hiking and cycling and the room to play basketball, soccer and roller blade. In winter, families bring their children out to the large hill next to the area where Cool Creek has an annual "stomp" and snowboarding and tubing is a common sight. Additionally, the Cool Creek Nature Center offers visitors a number of interesting programs year round and a concert series. In fall, everyone looks forward to the giant haunted location being the haunted trails.

The area around the park is interesting in itself. The bridge on Union Street just north of the park is still called "Cockeyed Bridge" even though it's been straightened and replaced. It was the site of the first car accident in Westfield. Additionally, on the north-east corner of 151st street, was a rumored speakeasy about where Thatcher Lane is. It was called "The Flame". According to a few long-time residents of the county, back in the early 1930s during Prohibition, even the staunchest man wasn't opposed to nipping down to the speakeasy. Westfield was dry and this location was closer than going to Jolietville.

Cool Creek Park on a good day is warm and welcoming. But when the shadows grow long and the sun begins to sink below the hill of 156th Street, it becomes a vine entangled, tree-scraper of hidden noises and strange shapes shifting through the darkening brush. When morning approaches, the same apprehension is apparent with an eerie quietness that seems unnatural.

One place this is apparent is the Administration Office. The beautiful brick and stone building was built thanks to a donation from the Legacy Fund made by Fannie and Leeland Reese. It blends in the dense trees and provides an outwardly comfortable work environment. However, not everyone is relaxed in the building. Several employees have had experiences, yet they remain reluctant to speak. Some employees are simply coping with the experience and others are afraid of what their bosses might think.

Kathy* came face to face with a spirit in one of the meeting rooms, she told her boss she was ill and left for the day. "I came in a little early to get a jump on some extra work." As I walked toward my desk, I passed the meeting space and saw a dirty looking man staring back at me." Upon closer inspection, she saw that it was indeed a white young man who looked as though he'd worn goggles and the rest of his face was black, "as if with soot". His tall, thin frame held up ragged pants and a longer shirt. His hair was dark and short, "Although," Kathy admits, "it could have been simply dirty as well." He viewed her with "dark, intense" eyes.

"I was so taken aback by what I saw, I could hardly get the words out, but I asked him what he was doing. He simply shook his head and vanished. " Kathy showed me her arm, "Goosebumps. What happened next was horrifying for me at the time. I turned to leave and saw him blocking my way to my desk. I went around and decided to wait outside until someone else arrived. I made my way back out and there he was, standing by the exit."

Kathy went on, "I felt very ill and my stomach felt as if I'd been hit. He started walking toward me. I didn't know what I was going to do. Suddenly, the door opened and he disappeared."

The oddest part about this exchange was that when Kathy looked outside to see who had opened the door, she found no one. "That was it for me. I left for the day and took a sick day. I don't know if it was some good/evil game being played out. I don't want to know. But, I haven't seen him since and I don't want to."

Joyce* had an experience as well but it didn't involve the same person. Joyce considers herself "pretty grounded". She admits her grandmother and mother are "somewhat clairvoyant" and she herself have had "experiences" on different occasions. Her experience in-volved being the last in the office.

"I wanted to finish some work and so I decided to stay late. It was a mid-winter's evening and so it got dark very early. I flipped on a light at my desk and went back to work. A few minutes later, probably about 30 or so minutes, I decided to use the facilities. When I returned, I found my computer completely shut down. I thought perhaps we had a power outage briefly, although I know that it should have come back on. I shrugged it off and got back to work. A little later, I heard a woman laughing in the hall. I went to find out who it was, as I knew everyone had gone home. I found no one. When I went back to my desk, my computer was off and my purse was sitting on the desk. I gathered up

my things and went home. I figured something wanted me to leave."
Hallie* also an employee had a similar experience.

Several people were out because it was close to a holiday and I was alone. I heard a woman giggle but didn't think anything of it. I thought someone had come in. Then I heard a child squeal, which got my attention and I went to investigate. I couldn't think who would have their child in the office. As I walked toward the sounds, I heard the loudest crashes following me. It sounded as if people were throwing heavy reams of paper or binders and banging on filing cabinets. I ran from the noise, which suddenly stopped. I stood in the hall for a few minutes trying to screw up the courage to go back. Finally I did. Nothing was out of place. I didn't talk to anyone about it because I didn't want anyone to think I was crazy. I've been there late since and heard the giggling again. That is usually my cue to leave.

The park itself has issues. Being in the ghost business, we get a lot of reports of ghosts. Sometimes people want investigations and other times they just want a friendly ear. Over the years several park patrons have related stories about their experiences at Cool Creek.

One volunteer was working the Haunted Trails event and was stationed at a rather large tree. The call went out that they were closing down for the evening. As she was about to leave, she heard a steady tapping in the tree. She doesn't believe it was a woodpecker. "It wasn't a fast tapping and it sounded like it was from the inside out, as if something wanted to get out." Another volunteer said she felt like something was following her. She acknowledges it could have been some sort of "critter" found in the park, but "it seemed more sinister."

A mother was at the park watching her children play on the equipment. A small boy came to her wordlessly and offered her a small orange ball. She smiled and took it, intending to hold it until she found who his parents were to return it. Her jaw dropped when she watched him walk away and disappear into the crowd of children. Turning to the woman next to her, she asked, "Did you see that?" The other woman had an "odd, scared" look on her face and said, "I didn't see anything."

Regardless of quiet feel of the park for some, for other people, the park will always be a dark place.

.

CAREY CAFETERIA

120 North Union Street

According to Helen Carey McColgin her family's business, the Westfield Cafeteria was open from the early 1920s until 1942. At the time, what is now Union Street was US 31. Since there was not much from Indianapolis to South Bend and people were always looking for something to do on a Sunday afternoon, "lots of well known people including governors" came to the restaurant. Additionally, prisoners being transported to Michigan City's correctional institution often were brought in for lunch. It was not unusual to see these men "cuffed to the tables".

But politicians and prisoners weren't the only famous people to visit the cafeteria. In May of 1934, John Dillinger and Baby Face Nelson came in with two women. They were riding in a Ford V8 and stopped at the Standard station (northwest corner of State Road 32 and Union Street). When the wanted men strolled into the cafeteria, everyone became excited. Oddly enough, no one moved to inform police of the wanted men's visit.

Legend has it that Dillinger came back several weeks later to eat on a fine Saturday afternoon, then he journeyed to Chicago to the Biograph Theatre. However, John Dillinger came back through and stopped at the restaurant – in a body bag. Helen Carey was reported as going out to see the body, just to see what it looked like. Some legends say she believed it was not John Dillinger's body.

The home the Carey family occupied was built around one of towns founding members, Asa Bales' old barns, and had no kitchen. As the family spent the majority of their time in the restaurant they also ate their meals there.

It seems that some remnants of the past remain in this building. When it was remodeled, a trapdoor was found in the main part of the building. While some believe this means it was part of the Underground Railroad, others believe it just means there is access to the pipes. Regardless, when an office was installed in the middle as part of a hair salon, strange things began to happen. The lights would go off and on in the evening. Many times the tenant in the other part of the building would think the stylists were working late, and vice versa, because of the lights coming on at odd hours.

Once, during the middle of the day, a shampoo bottle flew off the shelf. Eyewitnesses stated that it did not fall, slip, get bumped or otherwise moved by human hands. It flew from the counter into the wall near the door. A permanent dent made by the bottle was evident for many years.

While it was a hair salon, a crabby old man made an appearance in the office. At first, he was seen and would disappear. Then he began to mess with the business accounts left on the desk and he started to hide important documents. Finally, the salon owner told him that it was her space and he was no longer welcome unless he could behave. Although he resorted to making noises and playing with the lights, the owners items remained safe and no more bottles flew from the shelves.

Even earlier during the time the building was a cafeteria, often times, this same man was seen in the restaurant. It seems he was more satisfied with the food and company during that time. Some people believe the man comes from the original blacksmith shop that occupied the space before the current building.

In later times, the building was haunted through the phantom smell of sauerkraut, fresh bread and pies. In recent years, the haunting seemed to slow down. However earlier this year an older woman was locked in the bathroom. When she yelled to get out, no one came to her aid. Finally the door clicked, although it can only be locked from the inside. When she asked why no one helped, the guests in the business stated that they didn't hear a thing.

Recently, the building was vacated. It will be interesting to see if any renovations or change in ownership will affect this small, unassuming building.

The Carey Cafeteria building. Will the next tenant stir up the crabby old man?

AND THE STORY CONTINUES

I've lived in haunted homes the majority of my life. In the book "Haunted Backroads: Central Indiana (and other stories)" I chronicled the spirit-filled house I grew up in. Later, I lived in several haunted apartments, rental homes, and now, my very own haunted house.

Michael and I found our dream home when we least expected it. We were living in a home we were going to buy when numerous issues with the home left us with no choice but to move out. After a three week whirlwind home searching, touring and drive-bys, we were about to give up. One Saturday afternoon, we drove to the last home on our list. The ad had been attractive- landscaping, upgrades and a large lot.

We pulled up to the house, pretty happy with what we saw. Although landscaping was present, the yard was still a largely blank canvas to work with. When we walked in, we were ecstatic. It was a duplicate of a house plan we'd seen before but we couldn't wait for the house to be finished. This house, however, was ours.

When we closed and moving day was over, we were finally home. We'd just come from a haunted home and weren't expecting anything in this newer, one-previous-owner home. That night, we spent a good portion of time on the important things – like getting connected and making our first night comfortable. As Michael connected our computers and networked them, I made our bed and cleaned the bathroom (there really is *our* dirt and someone else's dirt!). I sorted through some small boxes to put things into their respective places.

To this day, I am completely unsure what made me look up. I know it was not a breeze, a noise or a feeling. But when I did look up from my place on the bed, a pale man with sandy blond hair and blue eyes was leaning against the door frame of our bedroom. He wore relaxed fit stone-washed jeans and a muted plaid shirt. His hands were in his front pockets, his nose long and thin. The man seemed to be in his early thirties. His thin lips curled into a smile at the edges. It was almost as if he were welcoming me. I couldn't see his feet from where I sat.

"Well, hello!" I greeted him.

Michael, who was in the next room in view of the door said, "Who are you talking to?"

"You mean you can't see the man in the doorway?" I asked, keeping eye contact with the entity.

Later Michael told me he leaned back in his chair and took a good look at the door. "Nope!" He declared somewhat cheerfully. "What does he look like?"

"Huh." I debated for a second before I answered, "He's as solid as you and I – "

And that was it. The smiling man simply disappeared.

That evening as we slept, both of us were awakened by the sound of something in the garage. We thought it was the boxes shifting. The noises weren't just a shift of cardboard. The ruckus we heard was outrageously loud. The sounds were as if someone were throwing the boxes, looking through them and discarding them. We could hear it coming up from the garage; we could feel the house vibrating. Neither of us wanted to investigate – but we did.

We expected to see a person, some sort of disarray or at the very least an animal, but on inspection, we found nothing – nothing moved; nothing tipped over. Nothing was out of place. Puzzled but not fearing for our safety, we went back to bed.

After that eventful night, we heard a variety of noises. Many sounds were attributed to the house. Others we couldn't explain. Habitually, our keys, phones, and other items disappeared. These items remained missing for days – or weeks in the case of a cell phone. The day after I bought a new SIM card to use in an old phone, my husband found the missing phone on the back of a chair – where we searched, cleaned and knew that it hadn't been before.

The sheer amount of occurrences was somewhat unsettling. In addition to the missing items, we had a host of entities move through virtually every part of the home. The shadows and misty figures that would move through the house became common place. Neither Michael nor myself were scared, rather we were amazed at so much activity. We were concerned about the kids, although I had gone through the house cleansing the kid's rooms. I also put the spirits on notice. The ghosts were not to scare the children or go into their rooms. For the most part, this worked.

However in our bathroom and walk in closet, the atmosphere was different. At one point, we had a pervy ghost who enjoyed watching anyone in the bathroom. We began to believe the spirits came from a portal. Many people and paranormal investigators believe that a portal is a doorway to another world, dimension or plane. When it is opened (through either the power of the paranormal behind it, a living person who is open to it or a combination of the two), spirits are said to travel freely to and from our world. Debate about portals among investigators and people with an interest in the paranormal exists, but not nearly as much as with how to close them or control the flow of spirits – if one can do so. As for our family, we chose to let the portal stay open and deal with each spirit individually.

We investigated the house several times. Near our walk in closet, we captured a faint mist forming After this particular investigation, our bathroom sinks would turn on during the night or be on when we returned from work.

During one afternoon, I had a feeling something was around. I began a conversation through dowsing rods with a spirit who told me he was a 14 year old boy from the railroad train that ran on the Midland trail behind our house. He wanted to be in the house because of my son, who was of a similar age. He missed his life but didn't want to move on. I tried contacting him several times after our initial conversation, but he didn't speak to me after our first encounter.

I began keeping a diary of events that has grown to dozens of entries since we moved in. As the years progressed, the portal in our closet seemed to change, and maybe even close. We do not have as many occurrences as we used to, although the house has periods of activity that we log. A favorite event was when I would do laundry. Many times in the dark, it would seem as though I wasn't alone. I blew this off often on an overactive imagination. Despite all of the activity in the house, I loaded our washer and returned to the kitchen. I left the light on in the laundry. Then I washed my hands in the kitchen and looked into the window, I could see the light shining in the laundry room. I also saw a dark shadow of a man pass in front of the light. I whirled to face whoever it was – to find no one in the house but me. I wasn't the only recipient of this activity. I was on a research trip to Richmond, Indiana one weekend and as I checked in with Michael one evening from my hotel room, he was speaking from his bed. He asked, "Do you know who walks around our bedroom?"

I indicated that I did not. Then he said, "Great. It walked to the side of the bed." I could only laugh and tell him to either interact or tell it to go away.

During another episode, I was bone tired one night. I crawled into my über comfortable bed and turned toward Michael and put my hand on his shoulder. I was enjoying my ride to dreamland when I felt something move the blanket and tuck it around my neck.

My eyes flew open.

It was obvious that it wasn't Michael. The kids were with their dad. I woke up Michael and told him what happened. He said, "Tell it thank you," and promptly fell asleep. I took his advice and spent the rest of the night in blissful sleep.

Other people experience the paranormal in our home. When my sister Lorri came to visit, she declared that there were several Native Americans in the trees on the Midland trail. They were protecting the land and the people on it. She had no idea of the conversations, investigation or the extent of our haunting.

A few years after we moved in, my daughter called downstairs and asked, "What do you want?" Michael, Christopher and I looked at each other. We said, "Nothing. What do you want?" That is when she said she heard someone call her name.

In 2004, Brittany brought in several items from her recently deceased great-grandmother. I recognized quite a few of them. As she brought them in, it was as if a wind of ill will was brought in as well. Her great-grandmother did not like me in life and I doubt her opinion changed in death. I really didn't want her items in my house, however, Brittany took her death hard and I could hardly deny her the comfort they brought her.

But the objects weren't to be as innocuous as they seemed. The house seemed somehow heavy and dark during this time. Shortly after Brittany brought in her items, I made macaroni and cheese for the kids. I have a gas stove and I am very cognizant of shutting off the burners. However, when I went in to clean up, the burner had somehow turned back on. Two weeks later, the same thing occurred. We were going on vacation shortly after this event, so as we were leaving, I told everyone to go out to the car and I had a talk with the great-grandmother. I simply told her if she was concerned about the kids, she should visit them at their dad's house. She was not welcome in my house and if she didn't leave, I'd get her out when I returned. Luckily, when we returned, I could feel that the house was lighter and her presence was gone.

In 2010, Brittany had another event occur. She was home by herself during the summer and she heard a noise in the kitchen. When she peeked in (as our floor plan is open) she saw a drawer in the kitchen open. A string that hung from the knob was still moving. In 2011, she came downstairs from her bathroom somewhat upset. She said, "I was in the bathroom putting on makeup and a roll of toilet paper was on the counter. I reached into a drawer for something and when I stood back up, the toilet paper was in the corner of the bathroom."

I looked at her questioningly and she continued very matter-of-factly, but I could tell she was somewhat shaken. "I don't believe I made it fall, but even if I did, it would have had to have made a turn to get into the corner because our laundry basket was in the way. And it wasn't unrolled at all. It was completely wound together." After this experience, Brittany asked that we reiterate that the ghosts are not to bother them, which we did.

Additionally, friends have had experiences- even when they haven't been in our house. While we were away for the weekend, friends dropped by to see if we wanted to go on a bike ride. They didn't realize we were gone and they knocked on our back patio door. Jose swears he saw a "white figure" move from left to right in our kitchen. At the time, he thought it was one of us, but when we returned, we told him we weren't there at the time of his visit.

As for Michael and I, we've still got our share of activity. Recently, we saw one of the ghosts on our Chatham Arch tour appear and then melt into a group of papers that were about her and her murder. Most recently, one evening as Michael and I fell into bed after a long day, something touched me most intimately on my ear. I giggled and told Michael to stop. He asked, "Stop what?"

For the second time in this bed, my eyes flew open very wide. Quite sternly I said, "Whoever is in this bed, there is room for two and only two, and these two are going to sleep. So knock it off." Again, I had a blissful night's sleep.

I can't wait to see what they have in store for us next!

This picture was snapped when we investigated our house. The kids and I felt something. When I took this picture, the mist appeared on it. We saw nothing at the time I took the picture.

SPIRITED SHORTS

Sometimes we investigate or are told stories that don't have a lot of history or information attached to them. For the first time, we're prepared to share some of these with you. As with all investigations and stories, they will always be works in progress.

EDUCATED SPIRITS

434 South Union Street

R. Peyton Cox donated some land between Cherry Street and Walnut Street and between College Street and South Street to build a school. Union Academy was first built in 1861 and became a major learning center for Quakers throughout the United States. At its height it had 200 students. Attendance declined at the turn of the century and in the Spring of 1911 the Academy closed. The following fall Union Bible Seminary opened with William Smith as superintendent until 1964. His son followed him as President until 1981. The Union Monthly Meeting of Friends was the owner of the building and rented it to the Academy until 1943 when it was purchased by Union Bible Seminary. In 1989 the name was changed to Union Bible College. Now it is called Union Bible College and Academy. The Estes House on the grounds was used for the hiding of fugitives from the South It is now used for storage and a bookstore.

I've always tried to respect religions and religious people especially in regard to the paranormal. I understand that some people and religions don't believe in the paranormal or believe the paranormal is really the devil in disguise.

I've spoken with many Quakers young and old and the overwhelming response is that they either believe or they don't – no different from any other demographic. In the case of one Quaker teenager who used dowsing rods on a tour, she said, "Oh, my religion is really cool with this kind of stuff!"

The oldest part of the building is from 1861 so it was no surprise when several students and members of the Friends meeting house told me that they had experiences. Below is a sampling:

- One student became very aware of another unseen person in the school when she went up the main stairway and heard someone coming up after her. She turned, expecting to see a classmate or an instructor, but instead saw nothing. As she turned, the footsteps went slowly past her and then ran the rest of the way up the stairs.
- The library is an amazing room. Several books date back to the 1700s. A student studying in the library was surprised

to see a child running between the tables. She asked the child to stop running around and a student asked her who she was talking about. They both searched but there was no child inside the library.

- An staff member said she was in one of the rooms when a breeze blew a 500 page book off a table. The staff member was adamant that the book hadn't been near the edge and the windows weren't open. "How do you account for that?" she was left asking herself.
- Sometimes the sound of a bell is heard during times when no bell should sound.
- Lights are seen in the upper floors of the building when no one is in the building (or should be!).
- Several town residents have seen what looks like candle light moving from room to room well after midnight

In recent months, the building are beginning to show their 150 year age and preservation options are being weighed. With whatever renovation or demolition occurs, I am sure the ghosts will voice their opinions!

Rich with history, this school has been a mainstay in Westfield for 100 years. Some of the ghosts have been here for almost that long!

BARKER HOUSE

Built in 1900, the Barker house belonged to the Olive and Russell Barker family, who had a gas station and garage in town. It has been remodeled several times over the years, most notably a comfortable living room was added in the rear of the home. The outside looks much as it did when it was built, and the upstairs still sports the original wooden floors.

Several owners report mysterious events in the house. Barbie* said her experience started when she was asleep on the second floor. The upper floor has two bedrooms. At the top of the stairs was a landing. When you move to the right, there was a small cubby hole with a door. Barbie would often feel as if something or someone was watching her as she slept. Once, she woke up to the rhythmic creak of the cubby door opening and closing. Getting up, she turned on the light in the hall and found the door firmly closed.

Other times, she would wake up and swear something was in the room with her. "I woke up and saw a misty black mass slithering out of the room." She explained, "I thought it was my imagination, but then I heard the footsteps. It started walking down the stairs. When it got to the bottom, the footsteps stopped." She went downstairs, phone in hand, thinking maybe it was an intruder, but she found nothing.

Finally, Barbie said that whatever it was enjoyed playing pranks. She would frequently hear someone walking up and down the stairs. On these occasions, she'd go upstairs and invariably, the little cubby was open. Although she'd explored the inside of it, the reason for the pranks remained a mystery. "I never found anything in it or found a any secret panels. I often wondered if anything was hidden behind it, but I didn't want to take the chance of letting something else out, you know?"

All too well.

The identity of the entities causing the occurrence remain a mystery.

DOCTOR'S HOUSE

When we were asked to investigate the house, it was because it had a "funky vibe" that the owners didn't like. Especially their pre-teen daughter, Janet*. She just didn't feel comfortable in the house. Luckily for her it was used as rental income for the family .

The house was built for a doctor in the 1880s using balloon framing, a method involving long studs that run the vertical length of the house with the various floors nailed to them. The only access to the attic was through a small vent plate on the outside.

Normally when Michael and I go into an investigation, we want to recreate what the phenomenon is. When there is none that we can recreate, such a feeling, it is up to us to decide what pot-luck methods might elicit responses. Additionally, we want the people experiencing the phenomenon to be available and a part of the investigation. After all, they are the people that are experiencing it, not us. Finally we want to recreate the conditions as accurately as possible, so we go in close to the same time the phenomenon is occurring. In this case, the feelings happened during the day and early evening. Janet did not tell us what happened because we wanted to go through the house unhindered and see if we could sense where these feelings were coming from.

Michael and I went in and took a tour of the home. We set up a few stationary cameras and let the video run. Michael was in charge of taking photos. I took a recorder around with the family to see if anything would speak. Finally, we conclude the investigation by having the girl tell us where she felt uncomfortable.

The girl told us her issues were in the middle bedroom. She felt very uncomfortable and occasionally she would see a shadow moving in the room. This was the only room in which we captured any activity. We have several pictures that include orbs in them. It was also the doctor's office.

Sadly, we were unable to continue the investigation. The house has been sold a couple times over. First to a business that sold antiques and a second time to a family that now lives there.

This beautiful old home was once a doctor's home and office. Perhaps the uneasiness felt is residual from a patient?

MINISTERS' HOUSE

The 2-story home had been used for many years for the ministers who worked at the Old Friends meeting house. Later, it was sold to owners who lived in the house for many years as well. When Debbie and Lee Harmon moved in, they lovingly rescued the home from the many layers of paper and paint on the walls. According to Lee, in some parts of the house, the paper and paint was so thick, the corners of the rooms looked rounded! Now the home is beautifully painted and furnished with unique privacy panels created and assembled by Lee especially for the tall windows of the home.

Within the first year they moved into the house, something strange happened. When Debbie's son Greg was in 4th or 5th grade, he was recovering from an ear infection. Debbie checked on Greg, who was recuperating downstairs on the couch. Imagine her surprise when she saw a red Mylar balloon from the Westfield Pharmacy travel down the stairs to Greg. The balloon, Debbie reported, had been in Greg's room. To get to the couch, it had to leave the room by getting through the doorway, turn several corners, go down the hall and then move down a stairway that has a low ceiling overhang about half way down the stairs. And then, it had to turn to get into the living room!

According to the couple, no other odd occurrences happened in the home, but it is definitely an event that even 27 years later neither of them will forget!

A red balloon made its way through a hall, down a stairway and into the hand of a waiting child.

OAK ROAD BRIDGE

Just north of 151st Street

The one lane 1923 bridge which stood at 151st Street and Oak Road was replaced in 2006 with a two lane wider structure. The area around the bridge is a remnant of the past. With horse pastures on either side, but with shopping and housing additions to the south, this picturesque road beckons to an earlier time.

The bridge replacement hasn't changed the fact that many people have experienced paranormal activity at this location. It happened to Doreen on an Indian Summer night. A bright moon played over the horse fields and shimmered through the trees. She had just come from a friend's house and was on her way home. What Doreen saw when she made a left turn from 151st Street onto Oak Road, made her stop her car. Directly in front of her on the bridge was a five foot tall misty figure.

"I blinked my eyes several times and yet, it was still there. I watched it walk from east to west. Or maybe I should say float. Just a wispy white shape. It didn't have the shape of a human, but it was almost like it was forming into one." Doreen's eyes widened as she recollected the event. "I didn't know what to do. I couldn't stop watching as it went across the road."

As the figure continued across the road, it began to lose shape from the bottom up. "It simply dissolved," Doreen shook her head. "I've never seen anything like it since."

NUTS TO YOU!

Corner of State Road 32 and Joliet Road

Although this is a book about Westfield, one can't ignore Jolietville. One wouldn't think it to see Jolietville today, but at one time, this small town was the place to party. Westfield was a dry town. Buggies, cars and people on horseback would come from around the western part of the county to drink bathtub gin in this mini-sin city.

The old general store was supposedly a speakeasy during Prohibition. The old building still stands, right next to the remnants of the old Joiletville bank safe, which John Dillinger supposedly tried to break into.

The store has had an interesting life. Started in the 1890s, it has been host to a variety of businesses, most recently the antique store and a private residence of sorts.

The antique store was a great place to browse. The owner knew how to price her merchandise in order to move it. Some of the best parts about the store were how it was packed to the rafters with *stuff*. Where ever you looked there was a shelf, a display case or a stand just begging for your attention. All items were organized, too. Even the back room and the loft upstairs contained treasures. I loved sitting upstairs in the magazines and books searching for that new elusive bit of history or fiction I didn't know I wanted or needed until I found it. If you were looking for a costume jewelry or antique furniture this was the place.

The former owner told me at first that she thought the scratching she heard was a group of squirrels, rolling nuts to store for the winter. Then, she began to hear footsteps up and down the stairs when no one was around.

One customer said she'd been up in the reading loft and hear the footsteps herself. She thought it was the owner coming to find her. She called out, "I'm up here!" and went towards the stairs, but when she reached them, no one was there.

Not all the noises in this building are creaks and pops. Some are footsteps from invisible feet.

TAKE THAT!

311 S. Union Street

The shop itself was a nondescript commercial building, remodeled for the shop on the inside and modernized with vinyl siding on the outside. Next to the old Midland train line, it was once the coal building for Westfield. It had also been a donut store and a grocery store with a questionable video collection on the second floor.

When I met the owner of a local hair salon, it was a cool fall evening. Like minded in that we were passionate about history and the paranormal, the first time we spoke was full of ghosts and history. Marie* finished up her customer and we spoke well into the night about the undead. Many times after that, we sat after hours in her shop, contacting the spirits around us, sometimes from the shop, sometimes from other places.

Often when I'd visit, we saw shape shifting shadows darting amongst the items in her shop or the lights would flicker. Sometimes, we'd feel hot and cold spots. What I found most interesting was the noise coming from the storage area on the second floor. Although it was packed, with very little available floor space, I heard footsteps walking above and down the stairs.

Once, a broom used to sweep up hair trimmings flung itself across the room, narrowly missing a customer. Several witnesses saw this event. The owner said with a laugh that she had a hard time explaining it away.

It is situated across from the Old Friends Cemetery. Sometimes in the evening, we would also see white figures moving within the cemetery.

This location, which is on our Westfield II tour, has always been interesting. On one occasion, a tour attendee took a picture of the building and three figures appeared in the photo.

Note: The Midland trail detours from the original train line in front of the building instead of continuing east-west as the original train line went through Westfield.

Once the Westfield coal yard and later a doughnut store. A seemingly unhappy spirit threw a broom across the floor in this building.

WHO ARE YOU?

136 East Main Street

Part of the original Westfield town plats, this Craftsman Four-square style former home has several stories attached to it. First, members of a family that lived in the home remember walking up the stairs to the second floor and seeing an African-American man with a half burnt face looking out of the bathroom.

A similar occurrence happened to another family living in the home. Ally, at the time a teenager, remembers being upstairs as well when the same man with a burnt face walked through her doorway and just stared at her. Ally described him as being about six feet tall with dark brown skin. "The left side of his face looked as if it had been burnt and the scars ran criss-cross over his temple, cheek, and over his eye." As a result, she said his eye lid drooped.

When she saw him staring, at first she was too shocked to speak. Then she said, "I started screaming for my mother. My mom and dad came up the stairs and tried to open the door. It was like it was locked. They were banging, asking me to open it and this man was just staring at me. Finally, he disappeared and the door popped open. My parents rushed in asking what was wrong. I told them what happened. They looked at each other and said, "We've seen him, too." The family was unable to find out much history about the house, however, they feel, with Westfield's Underground Railroad history that perhaps whatever had been on the land before had sheltered fugitives who had been abused by their captors in the South.

The house, which used to be an art gallery has recently been sold. Time will tell if the new owners witness the same apparition!

A man with a burned face walks through this house surprising and scaring people in the building.

THE 1844 CAREY HOME

136 North Union Street

The Carey family name is an old one in Westfield. Serving in civic and governmental capacities as well as charitable, the Carey's touched virtually every aspect of town living from the mid 1800s. Rose Carey ran the orphans home. Richard Carey was president of the State Bank of Westfield until the bank closed in the bank panic of 1929. Eli Carey was a blacksmith in the building in which Lowell Carey later ran a cafeteria in town.

One house that the Careys occupied was built in 1844 at the southeast corner of Union and Penn Streets. Believed to be a stop on the Underground Railroad, it has a hiding place in the basement. This spot is about 6 feet long and runs horizontal to the basement wall. During a home tour for the Westfield Washington Historical Society, Duran Designs opened its doors to let people see this area.

I was a runner for the day going from house to house and helping make the homeowners and historical society members comfortable. On one visit to the location, the owners relayed to us the idea that an older man is seen on the stairway to the second floor. According to reports, he stands about half way up and views the people working downstairs. Additionally, he's been seen through the windows during the evening.

Part of one of the oldest buildings in Westfield. An older man watches people from this beautiful staircase.

SECRET OF THE LAKE

US 31, north of State Road 38

The house is enough to make one shudder. An American four-square, it's been abused, used, and held together with metal, patches and luck, I suspect. Its most recent business venture was an antique store.

I love antiques – just thinking about the history of each piece and imagining what its seen is amazing. One early summer day, I dragged Michael into the place, as I think the more run down the antique store, the better. First, we dug on the books they always had on display on boards strung between saw horses and covered with a tarp. Although the books had damage, they were certainly a treasure trove and I took several titles in with me to the house.

When we entered, immediately the vibe was different. It was as if we'd stepped into the darkest pit of Hell. We circled the house counter-clockwise from right to left. A cash register with a small counter and some chairs were on the left. Three men sat silently and watched us as we walked. Large furniture was to the right. As we circled into the 11 o'clock area, we realized we were in what would have been the kitchen. They were clever in marketing as they put all of the kitchen items in that area. Commenting on certain items, we made our way upstairs. The feeling of oppression and panic had been building and it began to overtake me when I rounded into the first bedroom upstairs. It was a feeling of primordial dread as if something had happened, something that would have shaken people to their very being.

I was very surprised. I have always been somewhat clairvoyant when it comes to my family (not really for other people), but this inane dread was cloying and overwhelming. I made a surprisingly quick trip through the upstairs despite the amount of antiques to see. We paid for the books and Michael asked the men what the house used to be.
The men snickered and the oldest one behind the cash register stated, "It used to be a camp when the lake was still here." And that was it. Nothing else.

We said our good-byes and left the building. It was not as bright and sunny to me when we left. I couldn't get the feeling of dread away from me. I saw some rusting iron beds which unnerved me even more.

I couldn't get in the car fast enough.

When Michael and I wordlessly entered the car, we snapped our seat belts on. Without missing a beat, he backed out of the spot and turned to me saying, "I'm not going back there, and you can't make me."

"Why not?" I said, feigning innocence.

"Something is there. Something *unheilsam* and unhealthy there," Michael said incredulously. "Something bad happened there."

My eyes grew wide. Michael is a pretty easy-going guy who doesn't rattle easily. "Something really bad. Where were you creeped out?"

"All over really but in the kitchen and the room above it."

I was astonished. The same places I felt it. "Something bad, like death or deep physical hurt happened there."

We agreed that we would not return, but we did research the property. We found no proof of a camp nor of any strangely disappearing lake.

Note: Unheilsam means unwholesome.

THE CURSED BLUE HOUSE

415 West Main Street

Abel Doan was an early Indiana pioneer who first lived in Mooresville and later Westfield. He attended Union Bible Seminary (nee College) and married his sweetheart Phoebe (Lindley) Doan when he was 26. He did his best to be upright and to help his fellow man and the community. By all accounts, his life with Phoebe was good, although one son, Edwin, died at the age of 26 after being struck by lightning. His family bred cattle, sold dairy products, and raised nursery plants.

The Doan farm was situated between the current US 31 (Union Street is Old US 31) and Union Street from Main Street (State Road 32). The original Doan house is now part of the Conner Prairie Experience in Noblesville, Indiana.

After the land was sold, houses were built on it. One of the oldest houses left in the Abel Doan Addition, is now empty and for rent. As with many buildings in the area, it was many things over the years, from a rental property, to apartments, to a New Age store, podiatrist and dermatologist.

Although the origin of the original story related to us is uncertain, it is interesting nonetheless. A demon is said to inhabit the building. One former tenant complained of being awakened by a "pointy-eared blue-black figure with hair covering its skeleton thin body." It hissed at him and jumped to the light fixture, hovered for a moment and disappeared. "Afterwards, the whole room smelled like sulfur." The tenant reported this happening several more times until he couldn't take it anymore and moved out.

A visitor to the New Age store said she was looking at some items on the west wall of the shop and she looked off to her right. A similar creature greeted her. The bone thin spectre had pointed ears and was a blue-black color, as with the other sighting, but this one had razor-sharp yellowed teeth. She left the store without purchasing anything.

Still another visitor to the store recalled a similar apparition, but this sighting included the demon laughing deeply, running to the stairs to the second floor and scampering up them "as though he were enjoying his role and wanted to mess with us."

The origin of this phenomenon is not currently clear. Some people believe Satanic rituals were done in the house. Other people believe it stems from something "organic" with the actual land.

For now, it remains a mystery.

This house has been a variety of businesses and also apartments. The reason behind the occurrences in this building are an enigma.

MILDRED'S HOUSE

135 North Union Street

This 1901 American Foursquare used to be owned by Mildred Stalker, a life-long Westfield resident, until her death. Now it is The Fern and used for parties and meetings. The owners called in a paranormal team to investigate the building. The night-time investigation largely yielded nothing visible. As the team was packing up to leave and analyze their data, one of the investigators saw a black shadow cross an upstairs window, blocking the outside light.

Mildred Stalker lived in this home until her death. Now the owners serve up parties and food for various groups. People report a shadow figure on the second floor.

SIMPLE WHITE HOUSE

The ranch home looks innocuous, but that is hardly the case. Used as a rental, several tenants report noises and strange happenings. Dogs growl in the kitchen for no reason. Lights have been on when people return home, even though they were not on when they left. Footsteps are heard on a regular basis and doors open mysteriously. A former tenant heard an agonized cry in her living room although she was the only person in the house.

Some occupants believe there has been enough unrest from people moving in and out that troubled or restless energy has built up and is at a "boiling point".

This unassuming house on south Union Street contains very unhappy and active entities.

BELL RINGER

101 S. Union Street

If you look closely enough at the building that houses Union Street Flowers and Gifts, you can see the remnants of the large windows that used to allow patrons and people on the street to view the original location of Westfield Pharmacy, which moved to the building next door.

Since 1990 Union Street Flowers and Gifts has dished out gorgeous flower arrangements and unique gifts for Westfield and beyond.

Between the two businesses is a large door with a ramp. It makes moving items into the store very easy. On the door is a little old fashioned bell. Occasionally, the bell will sound when no one has moved the door.

This old drug store and the new one next to it were once a huge center of community activity in Westfield. Now, a helpful spirit inhabits the buildings.

VINE ALLEY

Between Cherry and Union Streets

An old blacksmith's shop used to be across from the McMullin Funeral. Many different nights people would see a white transparent man run from the blacksmith's shop to the funeral home and back again.

Some former funeral home employees and guests speculate the blacksmith may have lived in the house attached to the funeral home. We will probably never know.

The area has changed a lot in the past 20 years. Only two original homes remain in the area. The funeral home is now a parking lot. The blacksmith's shop was torn down in 2006. A cement slab and a carport mark the spot.

SURPRISE!

110 South Union Street

Nestled in the red brick building on Keltie's Restaurant is host to an upscale dining experience. Chef Keltie Domina and her staff try to make every experience for her guests a memorable and rich one. Her Sunday brunch is award winning and food such as Beef Wellington and unusual salads make Keltie's a destination spot in Hamilton County.

The building has not always been a restaurant. At one time, it was home to Keever's Hardware. Before that, it was rumored to have been a bakery, general store, and a jewelry store, but none of this can be established as true at this time. When it was Keever's Hardware, the employees claimed there was a "helpful spirit" who worked with them to fill orders for customers. On more than one occasion, as an order would be filled, the employee would come back to the front only to find other pieces of the order had been filled already- when no one else was around to do so.

The restaurant approached us to do a dinner tour a couple years ago and we happily agreed. We held it in the Fern in early October. As part of the tour, we brought people into the building so they could see the area of the haunting. We told the story and people milled about taking pictures. As we circulated around, an employee told us, " Ask the manager what happened in the kitchen." Always up for a good story, we did.

Ella* told us one evening the restaurant was closing and she needed to pick up her daughter. Returning, she entered through the back door and was very surprised to see dried muddy footprints that went from the back party room into the dining room and then into the kitchen. She called another employee, Jason* and asked what had happened. He declared he had no idea, as he'd just mopped the tile section of the kitchen and no one had been in the dining room since it closed. They cleaned up the mess and although stymied, didn't think much more about it.

A few months later, the staff came in to a similar situation. Instead of just finding dried muddy footprints in the kitchen and party room, they also found footprints in the foyer and up the walls as if someone had wanted to make a point. A thorough questioning of the staff came up with the same conclusion as the first time. There was no rational explanation.

Still even later, the same footprints were found in the party room and kitchen, but this time small dog footprints were found with them. They were the same dried beige mud.

Our interest piqued, we went back to John*, a customer from the hardware store and asked if he had ever witnessed any other ghostly activities happen in their building. He laughed and said, "Oh yeah, occasionally, I'd be there and I'd hear a dog yap and someone say 'Now, hush.' After a few minutes, it would stop."

Keltie's is focused on offering her diners a top notch experience with outstanding food, excellent drinks, and service that leaves you knowing what should be the standard. Although they do not dwell on or talk about the haunting often, who knows? Your next dining experience may be with another invisible diner or two.

Keltie's used to be a hardware store. Many people are still wondering who is leaving the footprints in the building after hours.

ORPHANS' HOME

Westfield operated the Indiana Children's Receiving Home from the late 1800s until 1906. The building was split into two homes sometime after it ceased operation in 1906. By all accounts, the orphan's home was a pleasant one. The institution sent the children to the same school as the other children in Westfield and it provided filling meals and spiritual guidance to its occupants. Additionally, when a child reached 16 or 17, he or she was guaranteed employment to make a living. Hank West, mentioned earlier in this book, was one of the orphan's who lived here.

Today, one part of the home seems to still have a small occupant in it. The owner hears a small child say "Mommy?" when her own children are still in school.

Meager records about the Indiana Children's Receiving Home are very incomplete. No records exist documenting deaths in the building, however, perhaps it is an organic footprint of a child that found it a comfort to be in the home.

An old postcard of the Indiana Receiving Home at Westfield. Later, the building was turned into two homes.

Half of the old orphan home on North Union Street. It is now a private home.

Half of the old orphan home on North Union Street. It is now a private home.

SOURCES

In addition to personal interviews, tour and investigation material, the author also used the following sources for background information.

"Army Spc. Luke P. Frist " Honor the Fallen 5. January 2004. Retrieved n 4 July 2011 from http://militarytimes.com/valor/army-spc-luke-p-frist/257007 .

"A Taphonomic Analysis of Human Cremains from the Fox Hollow Farm Serial Homicide Site." 2004. (Thesis abstract). Amanda J. Baker.

"Confined Space: Weekly Toll" 25 September 2005. Confined Space. Retrieved 15 January 2010 from http://spewingforth.blogspot.com/2005/09/weekly-toll_25.html

"Herbert Baumeister" Jospeph Geringer. n.d. TruTV Crime Library. Retrieved 15 January 2010 from http://www.trutv.com/library/crime/serial_killers/predators/baumeister/side_1.html

"History of Hinkle Creek Friends Church" n.d. Waldo Beals and Oliver Perry.

"History of Hinkle Creek Friends Church 1936-1986. n.d. E. Frank Burris.

"Hittle, Chad J." Indianapolis Star. 16 September 2005. Retrieved 15 January 2006 from http://www2.indystar.com/cgi-bin/obituaries/index.php?action=show&id=46753 Obit.

"In Memory of Chad Hittle 107" Facebook.com n.d. Retrieved 15 January 2010 from http://www.facebook.com/#!/group.php?gid=210866401357&v=wall .

"Model Mill building has a spooky past." 018 January 2008 Jerry Heaton Snyder.

LaPorte Herald Argus 10/7/1972, Robert A. Paskiet obituary.

LaPorte Herald Argus 10/9/1972, Robert A. Paskiet obituary.

""Natalie Wheeler Trail-Westfield" IndianaTrails.com. n.d. Retrieved 7 April 2010 from http://www.indianatrails.com/content/natalie-wheeler-trail-westfield

"Open Doors of Washington Township, Inc." Open Doors of Washington Township. 17 Janurary 2011. Retrieved 20 January 2011 from http://open-doorswashtwp.com/wordpress/?p=3 .

Our Westfield 1834-1984, Westfield Historical Society. WWHS.

"Robert King Victim Fatal Accident" 2 November 1931. Noblesville Daily Ledger.

"The History of Cicero". n.d. Unknown.

Weinstein, Fannie and Wilson, Melinda Where the Bodies Are Buried. NY: St. Martin's Press, 1998.

"Westfield Firefighter Dies in Crash" 15 September 2005. James A. Gillaspy. Retrieved 15 January 2010 from http://www.firefightingnews.com/article-NZ.cfm?articleID=1721 .

INDEX

I

J

K

L

M

N

FINAL WORD

The author loves hearing from her readers. If you wish to contact Nicole Kobrowski, she can be reached via email at customerservice@unseenpress.com.

She invites you to join the Unseenpress.com, Inc. Facebook page: **http://www.facebook.com/ghosttoursIN**

Nicole is always up for a good ghost story!